Angel & Hannah

Angel
& Hannah

A NOVEL IN VERSE

Ishle Yi Park

ONE WORLD • NEW YORK

A One World Trade Paperback Original

Copyright © 2021 by Ishle Yi Park

Published in the United States by One World, an imprint of Random House, a division of Penguin Random House LLC, New York.

ONE WORLD and colophon are registered trademarks of Penguin Random House LLC.

LIBRARY OF CONGRESS CATALOGING-IN-PUBLICATION DATA
Names: Park, Ishle Yi, author.
Title: Angel & Hannah : a novel in verse / by Ishle Park.
Other titles: Angel and Hannah
Description: New York : One World, 2021.
Identifiers: LCCN 2020042202 (print) | LCCN 2020042203 (ebook) |
ISBN 9780593134320 (trade paperback; acid-free paper) |
ISBN 9780593134344 (ebook)
Subjects: GSAFD: Love stories.
Classification: LCC PS3616.A7435 A83 2021 (print) |
LCC PS3616.A7435 (ebook) | DDC 813/.6—dc23
LC record available at https://lccn.loc.gov/2020042202
LC ebook record available at https://lccn.loc.gov/2020042203

Printed in the United States of America on acid-free paper

oneworldlit.com
randomhousebooks.com

1 2 3 4 5 6 7 8 9

Book design by Edwin Vazquez

~ for all lovers ~

Contents

Angel & Hannah

I am a rose of Sharon
a lily of the valleys.
Like a lily among thorns
is my darling among the maidens.

~ SONG OF SONGS

I.

Primavera
Spring

Pssst. Ven acá. Illuwah.
Let me whisper you a story.

Way back in the spring of 1993,
Hannah met Angel in the heart of Jamaica, Queens.

They were crossing Union Turnpike in da blue of the night
when they caught eyes. Froze like winter headlights.

It was shock at first sight, loud as lightning, da charge
between them nearly stopped traffic

as the city slipped away like a raw silk dress
~ stood two wingless angels, a lovely mess

but desde el primero, Love was put to the test.
Hannah kept Angel hidden from her strict parents,

nestled in his twin bed, imagined them a rebel
Romeo & Juliet

(the book slept dog-eared in her JanSport as she cradled
his head, & dreamt a wild new life: star-crossed, star-blessed).

Perfect

By second grade, Hannah learns how to please.
Sits first row, hand raised like a timid daisy.
96% on math, 100% on spelling.
Ms. Olive wants her to skip a grade.
Perfect, except when she turns mute,
when her eyelids droop like deadweights.
No one knows her father robbed her sleep,
kicking her mother at night. How she stood between,
a boxing referee, sobbing, *Hajimah! Stop it.*
Please . . . voice crumbling like chalk.

Next morning, her mother pulls Hannah's hair
into two high, happy pigtails. Clips her OshKosh dungarees.
Be good girl, Uma asks. *Yes, Uma,* Hannah says, voice bright
& thin as her classroom's sick fluorescent lights.

LITTLE SOLDIER

In second grade, Angel's a small, inept soldier,
shoved daily by Alex, one head taller, one year older,
who calls him Red-bone, Spic, Rice n' Beans.
Cokebottle glasses enlarge Angel's eyes as he finger-traces
words in *Lassie*. *Bark* becomes *dark*.
Consonants loom like pines.
He's sunless, compassless
in the last row's backwoods. No one
searches for him. Mr. Heller, lost in crosswords,
sips coffee. Snaps, *Will ya shut up please?*
All of you — heads down! Keep reading.
Under his desk, Angel breaks a pencil . . .
a quiet pressure of thumbs — crackk! —
Mr. Heller's head shoots up, a startled buck —
Who did that? Silence. Alex's spitball
grazes Angel's ear, a white bullet.

Before Angel

The neighborhood whizzes past her. Hannah flees.
Rides her ten-speed to the bay, air tinged
with gull-squawks and salt-wind.
A tongue of rock laps into water. She
walks barefoot over crevices, stinkweed,
a stone with Tony & Gina forever inked
in Wite-Out. A rat clinks past a Heineken.
She stares out to where the sky bleeds
blue into water, to the very edge
of herself. She wishes herself there. Past
the low slurp and suck of ebb & tide,
past Apa's backhanded slap,
fist choked with Uma's hair, where a crescent
moon thins like a daughter pedaling into air.

Hannah lies on a bed of books at night.
She enters them, portals to escape
the sad, repressed air of her parents,

she flies on a magic carpet of words
out the window over wild, lush gardens,
to fat gold pear trees. Leaps off fire escapes,
to moonscapes where a stallion huffs

and paws at the broken silver beneath
her hooves, she feels their ghost snorts
on her neck as she nuzzles them,
the stallion crunches fat green apples, words

like duende, hearth, tribe, flute her ears . . .
thin book ~ spines press against her spine,
and shadowy pages billow with her breath.

AVIATION

Angel goes to Aviation High School,
cuz even though he rarely leaves his hood,
he dreams of soaring sky high, a cool

legend in control of flight ~ he can
taste the sweet wind when he makes a fleet of paper planes
in class, but Mr. Heller misunderstands

his daydreams for disrespect, claims
Angel aimed the paper missiles to hit his balding head.
Suspended for three days. *Teachers are all the same,*

he thinks, while rolling up a Philly blunt.
He'll get his high another way now, blowing
O's of gray smoke out his kitchen window for fun.

Inside, he feels a small despair growing,
but keeps his guard up, no hurt showing.

QUINCEAÑERA

On Friday nights, Carina & Hannah drink Olde E's
on a peeling green bench at 109th Street Park,
till an amber, foamy buzz blurs the dark edges of night.
They watch boys shoot hoops like lean,

heartless seraphim, then test chain-linked swings,
Nike soles pointed towards heaven,
towards star-shaped leaves. Sometimes, she wonders why they
spend sunsets preening like two peacocks,

shadows huge on an abandoned playground.
But tonight, there's somewhere else to go, Tasha's sweet fifteen
in St. Mary's church basement. Hannah licks her lips,

draws on scarlet liner. She puckers.
Paints herself darker, more dangerous:
a girl who can scar in the shape of a Kiss.

CATTLE

Beyond flushed, sweating bodies,
pushing like cattle below black & buzzing speakers,
under a torn pink streamer
loose as a tendril of hair — lush —

his eyes. Darkluminous. Warm. A blush
floods her. Hannah sucks in her breath, but
can't pull back. Music fades. A hush ~
he's a young buck in the underbrush,

still in a disco ball dance of shadow & light . . .
all that Ever Is, Was, Will Be —
He. A deep longing floods her. And She —

black-haired raven, might startle, take flight at any breath. Leave only
a rush of wing. But neither, neither turns to flee ~

they stare boldfaced into Fate, or Destiny.

DANCEHALL

"Aquel viejo motel" . . . Hannah's weekly salsa
classes with Maria pay off ~ she spins
in a hot whirlwind

under his leading hands, already they speak
a language beyond words ~ movements, breath,
lust, stars, sweat ~ a circle clears

in the middle of the dance floor so they can turn,
dip, laugh, wink, grind, bogle, butterfly
beside, behind, & inside each other's arms —

DJ switches to Super Cat & she switches her backside,
grinding into his hips. She runs her fingers
down his neck, makes him shiver . . .

she grazes his temples with her fingertips,
she's breathless when the song ends.

LIVE WIRE

It's a throbbing pulse — live wire — this unspoken electricity
crackling between them like radio static ~ she isn't familiar
with this hair~raising heat, how it streaks thru her veins for him.

After Tasha's quinceañera, they stand outside,
in a loose circle with Beni & Carina, eyeing each other.
He keeps his distance, shy, but eventually offers

her some Juicy Fruit gum, asks her where she's from.
Beni is busy laughing with Carina as they walk
to the corner bodega. They slowly pair off in conversation.

She twirls her hair. He smokes a blunt —
politely refuses his offer for some.
But her number, she gives him —

    And under the blazing streetlights of Jamaica & Sutphin,
      he kisses her, soft, right on her lips, then disappears. She stands

                        ~ stunned in sweetness

Quiet

He's so silent, she muses, watching him
stare at the sun slipping into the sea
from the docks at South Street Seaport.
She loves his quiet, how deep & still he is;
an indigo ocean inside him.

his chiseled cheekbones show the sharpness
of his unspoken hungers, his eyes, deep pools
of the quiet sorrows he carries.
She laughs & talks constantly to fill da spaces,
her fears, her insecurities, the lacunae,

but learns to Still, with him — to relax
into the moment. Breathe. He doesn't say
much, mostly one-word answers. Never one for small talk,

he finds other ways to reach her ~ twirls a long
grass blade by her ear, tickling her, chewing its ends,
picking her up & carrying her piggyback down salty blocks.

◆

He's a little kid inside, rejoicing in play.
She lets her guard down, her petals unfurl;
lets her smile bring a spark of sunlit joy to his harsh world.

She feels safe & calmed by his quiet, lithe grace
as a candle cupped in two warm palms. She softly glows ~

Ay, mi Angelito.
Te quiero . . . te amo ~
mi cielo.

EL CANTANTE

Yo soy el cantante, and she is my Song, he sings,
a bit tipsy & slurred on his third Corona.
Y canto a la vida ~ De risas y penas
De momentos malos ~ Y de cosas buenas

Angel sings to her
to romance her, cuz words fail him
often. He used to stutter,
when he was little.

So he lets his lean, sinuous body speak for him
and instead croons a high falsetto ~
Y nadie pregunta, Si sufro o si lloro
Si tengo una pena ~ Que hiere muy hondo

Hector's words say it all, Esa Pena — so deep —

are there words for it in English?

PURE

He was red-boned, Taíno Indian & Boricua blood, lithe,
big, dark brown eyes like a child's, thickly lashed,
mistrustful, skeptical, mischievous, limitless ~ beautiful, watery, & deep.

Delicately handmade with iron wire.
Ashy until he shines with Vaseline lotion. He dreams of 747s
~ piloting sleek jets in pale blue skies.

Got fine cupid's bow lips, his eyes narrow,
high cheekbones glint when women act like players ~
stone~cold, gold diggers, rugged sisters

like his sister, who carry box cutters & brass knuckles,
who have bad habits that dust their noses white
while they scream at kids to *callate la boca* all night . . .

This one, she looks innocent, so pure to him!
He can tell she hasn't even smoked a cigarette,
a church girl~kind, but moves like Sin when she walks in.

Later that night, on his stoop, he exhales smoke~rings from his blunt
& in his mind, he replays his brave, warm kiss,
how they danced to his favorite song in unexpected bliss.

The first time Hannah visits Angel on his block,
he's not where he's supposed to be ~ on the corner
slinging rocks on his workday ~ he played
hooky to get a pizza ~ so all da familia

on Hart Street got a good look at his new girl —
She hears whispers from da stoops, *mira la Chinita*.
She sits on one in the hot sun, asks a tough-looking Tita
with a slicked ~ back bun, *Is Angel here? Why,* she say. *You his new girl?*

Angel saunters up, kisses her, and claims her with
his arm around her shoulder. Sun bright enough
to make them wince, they go inside a brownstone apartment,
dim lit & bustling with kids. Tita Angie softens, offers them arroz con gandules.

They feast. Afterwards, he holds her hand as they
watch *Tom & Jerry* with his little sweet cousins.

STREET RAT

Ay, he's a street rat, Wanda says.
Every homegirl gives her two cents
on Angel's dropout, drug-dealing
rap sheet. At lunch, Inez

warns her off Puerto Rican men:
Girl, they hit. They lie.
Got mad cheezes on the side.
Y celoso, not even romantic! Worse than Dominicans.

But no one knows how his eyes turn
her into legend, how his arms
shadow her like falcon wings . . .

In bed, words fade.
Only kisses, sweet as psalms.
No one knows his heat, his calm. His iron song.

LEAF

See her? She's tired of it already, wants to fly
or fall, dare gravity to break her. She's tightroping
her balcony, fingers outstretched like starfish grasping
for birch leaves and branches,
to steady her when she wavers, twists.
Leaves shiver like dried husks of vermilion angels.
They crown her hair
in a red rain. Far away, Donahue drones.
Dorito crumbs fleck the carpet like confetti.
Farther away, her uma sits, masked,
spraying rainbows on Glenda's acrylic nails. But out here,
God — saplings snap in her hands. Below her, a grass grave.
Her heart jackrabbits; she's balanced on an edge. Trembling,
no angels to watch her tiny, wild steps.

BOYS

Yo, she's gonna leave you, son,
Ariel slurs as he chugs his Cisco.
All these Queens bitches do — bet
— when she hits college,

gets a taste of those white boys
& their Porsches, their rich moms —
fuck that — you'll be old news.
That's why you gotta get yourself a cheese, son —

a queso on the side ~ women are like wine,
baby . . . Nah, nah, interrupts Jimmy. *They like*
Thug Passion — cheap, red, best when you drink a lot —

and yo, they fidduck you up!
Jimmy laughs, slaps Beni a low five.
Angel sucks his teeth, rolls his eyes.

DIME (ANGEL)

Why? Cuz she one of those good girls.
Straight A's in class,
but wild inside: can
down a forty like a man. Nice ass.
Chinita too. Never been with one of those.
Googie's boo wuz Filipina. She gave him two sons:
Mateo & Isagani. And scratches on his neck, son
~ she's a panther.
He'd catch wreck
for breaking night. He hit her.
But that old drama's not for
Me.
Hannah's my dime ~ small. pure. Shining.
She.

24

ARIRANG

In the old Korean song, one lover leaves another
on Arirang Mountain. *You won't walk ten li*
away from me without an ache in your feet,
she sings. Because that is the nature

of love: memories live on ~ make a home inside a body.
It's wisdom from Hannah's home ~ country,
from women who love in moon villages far from the sea.
When Hannah's mother left Korea with Hannah in her belly,

she stole that song across the ocean,
sang it as a lullaby as she bathed Hannah's young skin. Years later,
Hannah hums Arirang on her way to meet her first lover,

from the moon village of Queens to the moon village of Brooklyn.
April. *Aigu. Balam innat dah.* A fresh wind blows inside her.
Last night, the wind shook mimosas on Fifth
so she walks on pink petals to meet him.

BEFORE HANNAH

Before Hannah, Angel had crass,
blunt sex — once banged a girl atop a toilet,
ponytail hitting the rusted handle, once up the ass
of a thirty-one-year-old Mexican. Beni opened the door & laughed.

Angel hiked up his jeans and left,
threw a balled twenty on the flowered dresser.
Lust: a tequila shot he swallowed fast,
no chaser. Never had a girl who wept

black rivers on his shoulder,
kept her legs locked like stuck pliers,
kissed the cat-edges of his eyes.

The first Friday Hannah slept
over, she sat up in his bed, her eyes like small fires, she said, *Angel, let's be*
   more. Let's be real friends, too, You and I —

ROLLER COASTER

Hannah silently, steadily waits on Angel to call.
One day. Two days. Three days.
Finally, a ring!!! Sweet & lovely
to hear his hoarse, sandpaper voice tickle her ears.

A week or two will pass before she hears
from him again. *Is he a player? Did he get arrested? Is he*
alive?? She secretly frets, but when he calls again, she feigns coolness,
a lighthearted interest, when really, her whole being

is longing for another chance to be with him, to see
what he will do next to charm her, awaken her eyes, her lips, her heart, her hips.
This is what you get, she sighs to herself,
falling for a pretty sun-kissed boy with longer lashes than yours, girl.

She's drawing their names graffiti~style in her binder in art class already,
entwined with hearts, stars, & crescent moons.
So when I get to see you again, Ma?
He asks sweetly. *Soon,* she says. *Soon.*

GLOBE

They lay under the wink of the silver globe
in Flushing Meadows Park under a melting golden sun,
(she kisses his neck) they'd just begun.
(she kisses his earlobe) Reading Neruda's poems,
each word a hummingbird, midflight,
whirs silver ~ blue across the air —
her boy of flint and sinew, quietly despairs.
He sucks his teeth until he gets each word right.

His eyelids shudder every time they kiss
beneath golden-plumed cattails; his fingertips
fluid as they stroke and spin her hips.

She moves him too, those dusky afternoons,
whispering, *Tonight I can write the saddest lines,*
beneath the shadow of the world's falling latitudes.

KISS

Ay, who taught this boy how to kiss
like wind shirring a lake? His glinting,
lean, muscled boy~shape . . . Everything
he did with his mouth, a miracle —
how he slow-licked a red Popsicle

or rolled a Philly blunt, darkening
its skin with pointed tongue-tip . . .
In April, they bloom & kiss —

he grabs the wooden slats above his bunk,
hip bones grinding down. But lips —

barely grazing hers —
tongue~twirls. Quick
bites. He knots a cherry stem inside his mouth
& slips it in her mouth, O wicked gift!

FAITH

Why are they in love, you ask? Why does
water love sky? Moon chase sun? Light
reflect light? Maybe they love & caress

the hurt little kids hiding inside both of them ~
when they let the swagger down they let
tears. let song. let ache. let kiss. They give

each other space to dance,
to touch, to sing, to sigh, to burp, to laugh,
to stand proud (Pa'lante mi gente! Mansei! Amen), to collapse,
to hold each other sacred, sweet, & solid.

Some red ~ gold ~ fire chemistry ~
body alchemy & spiritual transformation ~
cultural education ~ they are in Love thru Space

& Time ~ like all star ~ crossed first loves ~ Divine.
Who knows why angels orchestrate this Love?
Trust it is Blessed from up Above. Amen.

WEAVER

O what a web she weaves! A dazzling
and intricate thread of lies and half ~
truths designed to keep her mom in comfortable
darkness, she'll say ~ *I'm studying*

at Carina's tonight ~ we have a test in math
tomorrow ~ I need my study buddies ~ please ~
her parents, overworked & underpaid immigrants, leave
her be. She commutes on bus & trains thru badly

lit, grimy, urine ~ smelling stations just to taste
one hour of freedom (~ Queendom ~) by his side, his hand
twirling her curls at dusk. She'll be home late

after she dances a few steps of salsa with La Fania All Stars
blasting on the boom box of his porch steps ~
mmm ~ a new romance sways in the sweltering heart of Brooklyn.

HANNAH'S PARENTS

(Pssst. Just letting you know, dear Reader, that sometimes,
these sonnets don't rhyme. Don't keep perfect couplets,
terza rimas, quatrains, or strict form, because Life often spills
outside da lines! Just like paint, just like pain, papi ~ just like

there are no words in English to describe to you
da Han of Hannah's parents ~ who carried memories
of war in their inner children, who as nail salon owners
would never have a chance to afford or go to therapy,

as they are country people of green valleys and full harvest moons,
all their golden beauty lost in cold white cities where their names
are butchered & mispronounced & made fun of daily,
while dollars still soften their callused hands. Hannah's parents,

overworked & silently missing Soju nights
with watermelon & squid anju & singing Arirang
& Sarang~ga with drunk, sloppy, & happy
Koreans who look & sound just like them ~ a kind of heaven.

They miss that, but cannot articulate nostalgia (Corea) to their born~here~daughter~
the beloved mother~land they left behind to give her this,
swinging golf clubs with thwacking fury over manicured green lawns
so perfect they make a man believe he has freedom.)

They come home when late-night Letterman
blares with canned laughter, long after Hannah
makes her rice & kim & kimchee rolls & tucks
her younger sister into bed, long after all the train rides
and bus transfers & taxi rides that transport their daughter
to the quiet pockets in the playgrounds,
seaports, beaches, corners, stoops, tree stumps that her & her lover use
as backdrops to their quietly blooming romance.

It all starts with a dance, she sighs, in remembrance, she
loves the way he always holds her hand &
pretends to lay out magic carpets in the rain ~
she feels a cartoonish, ballooning, indescribable joy with him ~
her secret, sweet angel tucked in the silver wings of Brooklyn.

TRAIN

She sings, *I will love you anyway,*
even if you cannot stay, echoing
Mary J as she waits for the R train,
voice husky as coarse grain.

Morning sun at Queensboro Plaza
casts slim white bars on the ground —
mute piano keys commuters pound
with shuffling, transient feet. *Are*

we all drifters, made of smoke?
She's on her way
from Bayside to Bushwick,

four subway transfers, two hours away. She
prays for the G to come quickly. She starts to sing,
when the train steals her song with its metal wind.

Rivers

It's always an adventure to go meet Angel. She prefers to travel
with a flock of her gold~hooped, gum~snapping, cute~curled girlfriends
for a double or group flirt~date instead of alone, becuz as a Chinita,
she has to keep her head humble & eyes down on da train,

not wanting to attract the glare of a jealous girl who may want to slice
her pretty cheek (slashings on da train were all da craze),
or a lurking subway creep. Sometimes tho, another boy
with a thick Nautica jacket & a sweet smile would slide

next to her, say, *Hi mami ~ where you going?*
And she'd have to balance friendly flirting
with a clipped response, strong but not too tough,
not enuf to be called a stuck-up b*tch or jumped.

Whoever he was would get a message when she said,
I'm going to see my man. Sometimes, they'd still escort her,
in that courteous, crowding way, until they finally gave way
when hearing Angel calling *Oooooh oooooh* for her down the street.

He reads her face in a second, *ay ~ telepathic!,* and she
can always tell when mistrust hardens his eyes. She rubs his shoulders
and runs her fingers slowly down the river of his lean, muscular back.

VIETNAM

Puerto Rican girls cock hips. Roll eyes. Suck
teeth. Bump her shoulder hard on his block.
Once, Vanessa screamed at Hannah, *Go back to Vietnam,*
bitch, then turned to Angel and sobbed, *Why? Why her? Why not me?*

Angel stood, speechless. For him, it was no better.
Stone-faced, balding Chinos on the 7 train
drill holes in his head. Frown. Cock, train
their mouths like handguns ready to spit at him. Or her.

Sometimes, Hannah shifts in her hard orange seat.
Sometimes she throws her leg over his, spits back a stare,
kisses Angel with rough despair.

At home, in the shower, they take time
scrubbing each other's limbs with care;
white lather, fingers buried in wet hair.

SAINTS

Angel always wore saints around his wrists
& neck. A gold cross & gold chain with Jesus,

escapularios & beads blessed by a Cuban babalao
given to him by his paralegal cousin Jessie,
and wooden bracelets painted with various haloed saints,

he's blessed with many. He gently slips
one off his wrist and onto hers . . . *mi amor,*
mi luz, mi reina, he softly sings, makes her feel blessed,

sacred, sexy, and sweet. She wears
his gifts with gratitude, changes her attitude
from shy to strong, from soft to bold.

When he's in the mood,
he traces her shoulder blades with sweet delight,
she shakes, shedding her scales

and blossoms into Woman in his light ~
grateful to be held & serenaded through the nights.

HOT CHIPS

They're splayed in bed, watching *The Simpsons*.
She's eating a ninety-nine-cent bag of Utz hot chips,
red dust coating her fingers. He's unbuckled, hips
thrust up. *Please.* He grins. *Please suck
it. No,* she snaps. *Not now. What
the fuck.* She swats him, but his hand keeps
seeking hers. *One minute. Ten seconds.* Her lips
curl into a grin. *Maybe. During a commercial* . . . his luck,
Cheerios bounce on-screen. She groans, wipes her mouth,
ducks down. His feet shoot up like arrows
at the ceiling. Then, he twitches, drools,
throws her off. *Stop,* he cries. *It burns! Hot* . . . *hot* . . . *hot chips!* Dashes out
her room, bathes it in the sink. *I'll get the milk*, she cries, and runs below.
    Ahhh . . . He sighs, and dips. She punches him — *that's what you get, fool.*

ADIDAS PRINCE

Underneath it all, Angel is a gentle man,
there's a patience in how he courts her,
kneels on one knee to tie her Adidas laces,

even in front of his abuela & his little brother,
Rafi. She blushes, touched, stirred by how he bakes her a chocolate cake
for her sweet sixteen, clenches a rose between his teeth. Tender lover.

She loves how his swagger announces his divinity
at weekend dancehall clubs — he'd hold her hand
and dance for hours with her at Latin Quarters and the Copa,

then hit after~hours clubs like two hot whirlwinds of beauty and grace.
She'd plan elaborate lies to meet him. Addicted
to da feel of his fingers, soft on her neck, his Juicy Fruit breath.

He rolls White Owl joints and blows clouds into her mouth
kissing her, tickling her, licking her, nuzzling her.
They keep each other happy, safe, and warm.
(Yes. Here Angel and Hannah ~ nestled in the calm before the storm.)

After I drop him off, I drive
home down Cypress Avenue
to the Interboro Expressway.
My stomach clenches at a tight turn,
a sharp fear of losing him
in this slick, lipglossed city.
A grainy dusk descends on all
car roofs, silvering them
into a black & white movie,
but I'm no starlet. God. I breathe slow,
clench the wheel, knowing I'll stay,
whether he hurts me, whether we
skid, flip, lie trapped in a box of flame —
my heart's strapped in, belt etched with his name.

HOME

Mi casa, tu casa, mi vida. Come. Stay with me.
Cada noche, he sings, *Let's make a home together, ma.*
We grown enough, yo. I want you Here with me.
Pretty please, mi reina. He bats his thick, lush lashes,

coquettish as a drag queen, takes her hand. Kisses
it, daintily, tenderly. How can she resist?
She giggles. *Ay, Angel. I'd Love to, cariño. Pero my parents . . .*
she sighs . . . *Look, ma. When you ready*

to be free ~ come to me. Estoy aquí. Esperándote.
They lay curled in bed like two commas
facing each other, quiet, creating
a heart, a nest, a space for Home.

No crazy K-drama,
stress, or tension, just a warmth, pulsing
like a rosebud about to bloom. *Sí,* she says,
and holds him dearly, like a mama.

I'm . . . (MIGRATION)

Maybe flying is in her
blood and bones ~ great-aunts & cousins
flying to America to escape the trauma

of the forgotten Corean war
that left her mom orphaned at five & changed her family's fate ~
burying Celadon vases & twenty-four-karat gold hairpins

in jars of kimchee, a hive of bustling, displaced cousins & refugees
her father took in, plus all his friends & neighbors (still alive)
arrive until his house swells, from eight to twelve to fifty.

His lovely wife dies of stress, claustrophobia, war, & poverty.
Hannah's mother runs from orphanhood, from a colonized country,
to escape chaos, grief, & molotov cocktails, to create
a new life, free of conflict, vicious spirals, struggles, & strife.

◆

It goes deep, kid. She could be running
from the violence her father carried from that war too, into
his body, into his home, buried

rage from leaving a country stolen &
conquered & raped & pillaged by
the Japanese and then Americans, fake friends

42

who took & took & used the same old divide
& conquer formula to occupy one half
of their divided country for more than half a century. What pride

can one truly carry when one is country — less?
All these Korean Americans, cut in half, divided inside, then hyphened —!
surviving, trying to thrive in the land of the colonizer ~ sigh ~

Bob Marley say, *You're running & you're running
& you're running away, but you can't run away from yourself . . .*

◆

She's running from a broken home,
running from her broken home-land,
her cold orphan mother & her divided mother ~ land,
cut into two sides by Russia and Amerikkka, and

she's running into the arms of the first man-child
who's ever felt like Home,
who makes her soul feel less alone,
good to smell & warm to hold.

She's running from her parents, who are mute,
who suffered so much they refuse to speak about Why ~
(but that simply creates another Divide
that I bridge for You, dear Reader, but imagine

how lost! how empty she feels inside with no stories, maps, mirrors,
or songs to guide her in this new world).

She Inherited a rage that lives
like a bomb in her body —
she inherited da stones of Han, and is spending her life unloading them
from her bowl, to become Light enough to take flight and disappear.

RICE GRAINS (HALMONI)

Aigu, gunyun bah. She's a disgrace —
a shame to the whole Shin family.
Look at her, kissing that black boy,
black as burnt rice. Look!

I want to scratch out my mound grave,
cross ocean, slap her cheek,
make her kneel on a bed of rice grains.
Whip her calves with a pine switch
until she bleeds bloodseeds.

Daughter of my firstborn son, born
on foreign land, can't even hold

my words in her mouth without spilling
them like wellwater . . .

she needs a living halmoni to slap her sane,
make her respect her family name.

7TH PERIOD (HANNAH)

I wait like a tiger lily in an overrun
garden, trying hard to be hidden
yet dazzling, fixing my burnt, frayed

hair. Late, he saunters over,
sharp as a grass-blade. When I lean
against him, a stiff bulge in his Polo
jeans turns me dew-moist. I learn

too late it's not his heat, but a silver .380
he uses to kill stop signs with a hunter's
flair in weeded corners of Queens. A peek

of silver-blue, he puts my hand there.
Hard. My girls stare. God, I long
to glint. Cock the trigger,
game for anything.

PRIVATE DANCER

The door's locked. *Put it on,* she dares,
flings her Guess denim-lycra dress
at his feet. He sucks his teeth, *nah.* She caresses
his earlobe. *Please.* He huffs . . . straps off buckles. She
stares as he struts from dresser to bed with a bony hip-jut,
arm extended like a thin brushstroke of tree.
He bats foxy lashes to throw shadows over his cheekbones, puckers lips, runs his rough
palms over her décolletage, then strips
further. To her cherry-red negligee. Totters in fake heels,
flings an invisible boa up at the ceiling. She
laughs, imagines feathers swan-diving past her eyes as he
skips over now. Done with fantasy, he kneels
beside her. Hard. Naked. On his bony knees.

ONE TREE

Hannah wants to take Angel into dark woods,
away from his bleak block with its one thin
    tree — god, one tree! Sick
smell of needles and burnt, cooked crack.

If she could, she'd hike him up the Catskill trails
her mother led her through as a girl,
    so he, too, can smell sweet loam,
let his feet find path through stone,

    leaf, root, each step Godsure . . .
to stretch his wingspan wider,
beyond the wire mesh of Hart Street's

metal aviary ~ Hannah daydreams
lounging on a milk crate, as Angel
hustles coke under the oak's weak shade.

TATTOO

Ay, who could not adore such a soft-spoken sweetie?
Left shoulder blade tattooed with a jester,
mouth full of hilarious smut — *Hey, let's take a shower,* he entreats,
my tongue'll be the sponge. A gum-snapping

goddess of Lust winks over Angel's bed, agreeing,
Love is the funniest! She lures
the two to locked bedrooms. Alas ~ in a few, he cheats.
So, she cheats, and they brawl, and Angel gets locked up.

Hannah works late shifts to pay his Rikers bail.
Far away she hears her mother's voice,
forcing her awake — *You can't save a lost boy* —

her breath sounds hot & stern.
But young lovers scar hard and take
each other's hearts for ransom. They appear
so cool from afar . . . up close, their small hands shake.

GRADUATION

South of campus, Angel strays
behind a mimosa tree, blurred
like a sepia photo, a secret.

Hannah bobs in a sea of royal-blue
caps & gowns. Angel frowns

down at his two-dollar bodega-rose.
Everyone's armed with exotic bouquets —
calla lily, iris, tulip. Angel

breaks a thorn off his prickly stem.
Hannah's handed her diploma onstage —
his throat stirs. She smiles,

hugs an oldwhitelady tight,

and snaps pictures with her Kin,
miles away from him.

JONES BEACH

They trail behind his cousins on the shore, till Chino
becomes one black speck, Jessie, another. Stripping sandals for fun,
they run barefoot into ice-blue, see-through, sailboat
water, no seaweed, dirty needles like Orchard Beach

or Beach Ninety-eighth, Latin Kings with black-gold-black
necklaces glinting on collarbones like silent threats to Nietas.
None of that old danger — just water, up to their chests.
They reach a point where their toes don't touch the sand.

Dip in and out of salt, their breath ragged now.
The undertow yanks their thighs with her cold hand,
grips them down, down, she panics, to death —
Hannah gasps. Sinks. Angel grips her neck —

throws her up and forward — *Swim!*
Onshore, they choke up liquid ropes of ocean.

Angel. Angel.
You saved me — she admits.

EDEN (HANNAH)

with you i'm not a girl
with small duties file
cuticles carry groceries
with you i unfurl

like Eve i can kill or heal
with my mouth and hands
turn a bed into a lightning-
filled tent steal

deep inside your
skin bloom stars
inside till you smell
like me

i burn like you kin
to our blood's
desire to flee from
Eden

VIRGINITY

He *ooo-oohs* her in DeKalb's train
station, takes her hand, lugs her JanSport bag
all the way to Hart Street in Timberlands, do-rag
tight round his forehead. Her hair, a horse's mane

dolled with spit curls just for him. She lies
to her mother, says she'll be praying at a Korean church
retreat. Instead, she kneels before Angel for her First
Time in a white peekaboo nightie.

His mother, Alma, lays in the sickroom next door.
Blue light falls over their skin in strips.
He kisses all ten of her chipped toes. Her hip bones.

The wooden floor begins to creak. She winces.
Clenches her fists into yellow rosebuds, stuffs her mouth with a pillow,
so his mother, next room over, can sleep.

Mute, she takes her first lover.
It has to be this way, no other.

SUMMER BREAK

Grains of light sift over Wyckoff
Avenue, dusting strollers shoved

by thick-hipped mamis with slick, gelled hair.
Tattered triangular flags blow and click
like sharp teeth above all heads.

Angel struts, clasping Hannah's fingers.
A cool wind ripples his undershirt,

dares to lift her skirt. Young fools with easy
grins, they stroll loose-hipped down Hart
Street, say *wassup* to boys ribboning D's Phat Beatz, Sal's Pizzeria.

Young street king and queen; everyone knows
his name: *Pssst . . . mira Angel y la China,*

they hiss. But the two own the block —
walk straight into a hot wind.

I slept but my heart was awake.

Listen! My lover is knocking.

~ SONG OF SONGS

II.

VERANO
SUMMER

For now, these hot days, is the mad blood stirring,
lives churned & cut like 'copter blades whirring

across a bleak Bushwick sky — Hannah's disowned,
left with only Angel's arms for a home —

Rafi snores between them in the cramped twin bed,
they're more than lovers now; they're surrogate parents.

Deep in Bushwick, they decide to rent a small one-bedroom,
cook pots of arroz con pollo together and soon,

warmth spills into their lives like a late noon sun,
but the beauty dries out almost as soon as it's begun,

cuz Angel's fam crashes at their crib, makes a mess of it,
Hannah throws clothes, plates, hour-long bitching fits —

they inherit the sins and vices of their folks, no heat,
their hearts & apartment grow cold —

they cut each other to bone / no more tenderness to bleed —
like a hot wind, she scorches his earth and leaves —

SPLIT

I'm leaving to live with Angel, Hannah says under her breath. Her father sits with fists
clenched on the kitchen counter. He twists
his mouth into a sad grin. Her mother waits,
gripping doorway. She prays
her husband won't kill her daughter, grab wrists,

bend them into mercy, bash his fist
into her baby's baby skin. He takes
a whisk from his blue inhaler. Air is hot, un-
bearable, thick . . . *If you . . . disown me, apa, I . . . I
understand. But I can't . . . stop . . .
loving this man.* Hannah weeps. Presses
her hand on her apa's knee. He drops
his head. Sobs. *Why . . . why me?*

MOVING

She packs her dresses while her dad's
at work. Slams CD cases till they crack, white lightning down Mary's face.
Doesn't stand & look at white
bedroom walls, no, it's all done in a hot rush,
fire burning her Nikes
to get the hell out. *Fuck this house,*
she seethes. House of broken plates,
torn hair, han, misery.
She shoves handfuls of socks, quarters, thongs into her JanSport,
watches the clock, calls Four Twos,
looks back out at the quaint,
two-story wooden houses,
bird-filled, tree-lined streets.
No one sees her leave.

GRACE & GRIEF
(HALMONI)

There she goes.
Another split.
Split nara, split family.

Is our fate a legacy of
grief? A history of han
for eternity?

My ancestral tree
shredded like
rice paper

in a hard immigrant wind. Aigu.
Wild girls —
what mother-pain!

She's my penance — she's
me, fifty years later, still hardheaded.
Stunning,

headed straight for
tragedy she thinks is Love
or Destiny.

But to spit her
into the city-jungle,

among ghosts, demons,
thieves? No place for a
jashikeh. Aiyu. Look how
my son and his wife salt
& smoke in separate
rooms. Tombs. God, what
is this world?

Are we all guaranteed moments of grace
as well as grief? Little girl-fool, I bless you
tonight with a sorrowless
sleep,

but tomorrow —
and beyond, Hannah-ya

what you sow,
you reap.

KNICKERBOCKER

Hannah's first day in Bushwick:
sunstars wink on car roofs like gardenias.
Wind flaps tabletops.

Out every open window, Jerry Rivera croons.
Hannah sits outside at Sal's pizzeria.

Her skin and the brick, warmed red.
She watches two Latin Kings flex.

It's a new town, new smells. Adobo, saltlust.
She's see-through, an outline waiting to be colored in.
Please. One moment a day —

en paz — a light, cool wind.
Today, no evil.

Even El Jefe gums a tune
as he rattles down Knickerbocker Avenue.

HOME?

Funny. Here, in Maria's cramped bedroom
with its bare bulb & peeling walls, a rat
scuttling by lil' Juanito's minibike, three fat kids
plumped underneath her like pillows,

Maria stretched out like a queen in short-shorts

popping seedless green grapes into every
kid's open mouth, Tito's laughter,
window open to car screeches,
slaps of Bereco's & Angel's domino tiles,
clink of distant beers, an iron bar
in Hannah's stiff spine melts . . .
she softens here, is almost home here,
nestled in chaos,

a fawn hidden in high grass.

FLOCK

One reason she loves living in Brooklyn
is everyone's kids: Alejandro, Joey, Sofia, Kayla, and lil' Juanito
flock to her like tough, cute, baby gray-
gold ducklings. Angie's youngest one is a lost starling

adopted by the young and scrabble-beaked.
They sing her Aaliyah songs, clamber over her shy frame,
pluck tufts of fluff from a futon couch to decorate
her hair with a tiara of wool and feathers.

Hannah does her homework while da other girls sniff & smoke,
watch old *Tom & Jerry* reruns & new Disney classics together,
whirl kids like tiny planets over the living room.
With small hands they drag her into bunk beds,
make blanket forts & play, far from the hard-eyed titas in the kitchen.

She feels blessed when Alejandro's tiny feet slap like webs over linoleum. *Titi!!*
He stretches baby arms towards her neck. She flies him up to kiss his brown ringlets.

DISCO

Angel, you are hilarious,
she giggles, spellbound, laying
nekked as he winds atop the mattress,
grinding hips like clockwork —

sssst!!! He sizzles, *chile,*
when a melody hits him
one Junebug afternoon: a distant reggae tune
thru someone's speakers like *action, tender satisfaction* —

mmm, Angel, you crazy!
he closes his eyes & slow-dances himself, magic —
he brings disco balls, confetti,
his body's pent-up sadness,
unwinding in a serpentine, one-man show. He throws

off sparks seen from a passing L,
soul-light gold as a summer sun
melting down a brownstone window.

HEAT

friday nite on Hart St!
hot enuf for kids to loot a corner hydrant
for its rainbows with josé's wrench,
rivering gutters, girls drenched

in tight tanks with curly hair
slink by while boys hiss,
ay Díos, madre mía, Cristo Santo,
as if saints laved in starry half-light can't
compare. out on his stoop, Angel passes

a strawberry Bacardi breezer to Hannah,
watches her roll it over her chest,
collecting beads of nightsweat.

he breathes slow, thick,
paws his sneaker against brick
wall, pushes towards her,

soft-licks her damp neck.

Under a hot night full of
bullets and flags, we sleep
in projects etched with
coarse pencils,

my red-boned angel with
twitching haunches, lean-
flanked — eyelashes lush
enough to net nightmoths
to keep them from waking
the calmdeath of our
calmbreath —

as I patrol shadows & silhouettes alone,

heater hiss like a
viper coiled to my right — I
am tiny,

cold-handed, brave
— I will cut you open to keep us
safe.

CYCLONE

Late July. Angel, a shirtless Pied Piper,
  leads a straggle of kids to the F train —
    Rafi, Kayla, Nicky, Sofia, and Desiree
      cling to poles like a cluster of robust grapes.
      At Coney Island, Angel rubs baby oil on Hannah's
        gold shoulders. Behind them, the old Cyclone looms.
          Kayla & Rafi bury Angel ~ pat-pat-pat in lumpy sand.
          A plastic cup leaks lightning-water on his torso,
            and Angel erupts, half-man, half-volcano,
            grabs a kid under each arm, two footballs
          he touchdowns in water. Hannah follows — he gives chase,
        she screams, her feet slap saltwater beads into her braids —
      she scampers, laughing past the Ukrainian hot dog lady
    who smokes & grins, mistaking them for family.

MUSK

Half-wilting in summer heat,
Hannah insists on silk dresses, pink barrettes.
Part of her is young, green, vain,
causes boys to drop jaw, whistle, swivel.

She's drunk off her own scent.
Angel's a pirate-paladin ~
pure, deadly chivalrous. When Sitta jeers
a nasty slur on the side,

Angel flicks a box cutter for her honor,
ready to kill, gut, die. Hannah reins him
in ~ *No, not tonight, babybaby.*
Please. He's not worth it.

But you are, Angel says. She smells his sweat.
She's damp, her panties wet.
At night, she kisses his temples,
drinks his musk, as he takes her.

                                    Again & again.

SUNSETS, SONGS, PEARLS

Mmmm ~ slow down all the moments
she has his head to her chest at sunset,
nursing him, mothering him, consoling him, stroking his fade
trying to keep him from killing himself slowly, fading away

into grief or pipes or blunts or beers or rage —
she holds him, and he holds her. Babysoft tender.
Stroke each other's hair like bold kids,
like first ~ time lovers.

Angel, ay ~ he loves to sing into her ears!
His high falsetto crooning Marc Anthony
or Jerry Rivera classics by her baby hair ~ *"aquel viejo*

motel" ~ or *"cara de niño, con alma de hombre"* ~ they hold
each other precious as gold Tahitian pearls
in a world that doesn't value their true worth.

Cocolivio

cocolivio one two three
one two three one two three!
how easy it used to be to fling
your arms round a pretty

young thing, squeeze tight as
a balloon right

before popping, no breath,
just you & her, hot, panting,

other kids blown like
dandelion dust

over tufts of dry grass
till googie's mom window-yells,

angelito — déjala! cuídate!
and you let go, run free — a
car barely misses you
gunning Hart Street —

Running! Christ, he gets stopped for running down
Wyckoff Avenue at 4:00 A.M.
by undercover cops who shove him,
spread him, grab his balls, pat him down

against brick. Officer Sanchez frowns
while Angel shakes his head and says,
*I'm late for work, man. I load trucks at Boar's Head,
near Jones Street.* They let him go, the sound

of tires slick against wet concrete,
their sirens stupidly wailing. He gets
to work — but too late. They let him go. He trudges
home. Slow. Kicks a soaked garbage bag. Spent.

Rain pelts him in hard sheets. Sleepless,
jobless, again. Four days left to pay this month's rent.

ABUELA

First time Angel takes Hannah
to his abuela's, Hannah knows
it's special, cuz he ironed
a button-down shirt & Polo khakis.

They step light into Paloma's fourth-floor walk-up.
Hannah sees glass beads, chipped ceramic
Jesuses, a plastic-covered sofa, blue gurgles

from a dank aquarium. *Mira,*
says Paloma. *Ven acá. Hola,*
señora, Hannah tries. *Ay!*
Hablas español!

Paloma's smile widens
to flash gold,
two crescent-moon eyes.

COCHO

Cocho burns buildings. His lazy eye
is red. His laughter, metallic.
Hannah listens as Angel's cousin brags —
how he doused a tire, rolled it into Boar's Head,

where trucks dock at night — a scratched-out
section of Bushwick, no lucky numbers, railroad track eaten
by asphalt. Hiss of lighter fluid. Fume. All dead beef burning —
it maddens the sky with rank smoke.

All windows south of Williamsburg slam shut.
Hannah nightmares: she's a blackbird
over a burning Brooklyn, a copse of tenements
licked in blazes . . . below, Angel, a cheetah
singed in flame . . . he looks up. Bares fang —
she caws . . . this far, he can't hear her cry his name —

No.

Why? Why not? *I can't. I can't do it*
anymore, Angel, it's not glamorous,
not sexy, not cool.

To bolt outta bed 4:20 in the morning
cuz a gunshot or a junkie stumbling
on our fire escape, a hand trying to unlock our
bedroom window . . . no. No more madness. I can't
breathe, can't relax, can't think!
Don't feel safe. We all want outta

this place, we all want
Grace. It's not you. Baby.
It's not me.
It's the city.

Look.
Please.
Look at me.

BUSHWICK

Every part of Brooklyn has a motto ~
Do or die, Bed-Stuy; Brownsville, Never
run, never will ~ but here, *Buuuushwiick,*
stretched long as an echo or a prayer or a dream

in nightclubs like a low hum ~ to counter bullet-
like chants of *L.E.S.! L.E.S.!* Bushwick is my heart
— this little place across da bridge, navigate
backstreets & deserted alleys & run

smack into her ~ she slaps you awake with her
sass. Gold-hooped lindas and brass-knuckled boys,
Latin Kings & Nietas with gold teeth and holy beads,

I know these blocks ~ these blocks own me. I
can walk down any street, duck into a doorway,
get fed a hot plate, get laid, get high, get dry.

◆

Bushwick. A state of mind. Que bonita bandera,
boricua ~ Puerto Rican flags draped on rusted
fire escapes rustle like stars do all night

in Aibonito, Abuela says, trying to dance & be seen
thru las palmas, and some old hero named

José Martí winks, nailed to a wooden beam

in Tío's makeshift candy store, at the sad, jangly
chords of the tiburón Pedro

(not Navaja) crooning jíbaro cantos on Lucky's
busted guitar, borracho, Abuela shaking her metal
maraca, Titi Lilo ululating to shake spirits

out da rafters, bare bulb dangling, clapping
to a homemade, Taíno-tainted, conquistador-

stained music that crescent-moons abuela's eyes.

◆

Lazy Sunday. Paloma remembers la isla to Hannah
in her laced-up formica kitchen,
draining sweet Bustelo coffee thru
that nylon sock, wiping hands on her blue apron.
How in Aibonito, Abuelo used to hack cocos
on her front step with a machete
so her nietos could drink sweet-water
dulce, tan dulce, straight from its brown cup
(before he left, the cabrón, she laughs),
and not far away, Las Tetas de Cayey, lush
mountains dubbed such cuz

they swell like two round
breasts ~ *ay, men,* Paloma sighs.
Can't they think of anything else?

JESUS

Too many Jesuses. Angel's getting restless —
left leg shaking, hunched over joystick.
Jesus on the calendar, glowing Jesus on the wall, mini-Jesus
decked out in robes & cane, herding sheep on top of the dusty tv. *Let's*

go. Let's be out, ma. He catches Hannah
on her way to the bathroom. *Why?* She sucks her teeth,
motions out the barred window ~ *Just*
cuz. She groans. She knows. Blue sky. Wind. He's a

pent-up lion, needs to prowl
his streets, stalk territory, be game,
be prey, be chased, give chase. Be live. Be wild.

But Hannah likes the cluster of saints
on shelves, old lace tablecloths, warm~gold
light, and most of all, Paloma's winking smile.

LOVE 101

These are the ways you love a man, in the details
~ cooking his eggs well done,

but not burnt, moving his radio to the shower
cuz you know he likes his Hot 97 in the
morning, drying your feet before stepping out the tub

cuz he can't stand a wet floor, letting him hold open
all doors, walk on the sidewalk facing street for some
chivalry that says, you "ain't for sale," dealing with phone bills

& unopened junk mail, kissing slow, from crown to
toes, all 126 of his freckles, his 22 scars, telling him,

~ *I love you, under-the-star-you* ~ never teasing
his too-early-to-be-balding temples, popping his pimples,

watching his eyelids shift in sleep,
moving closer, like you're his, for all Time, to keep.

Cocaine & Cheeseburgers

Cocaine or cheeseburgers . . .
Hannah laughs watching Angel half-nelson Ariel

& spray him with a Super Soaker between
customers in the midday lull. She tries math —

one week flipping burgers is 40 hours
5 bucks an hour x 40 is 200

minus taxes = 130 something . . . he could rake

that in, no sweat, hangin on Crescent, slinging bundles one
Tuesday, no managers, no egos, funny hats, just his tíos,

and Alma gets fed, gets quarters for loosies,

and Angel's left enough for tokens, movies,
weed, & my late-night cab rides to Queens. She sighs

as she watches him sell another sly handshake.

. . . how can you beat that and argue for Mickey D's?

HUNGER

After working on an empty stomach,
Angel looks forward to Tuesday nights
when King palms him his jackpot —
a bouquet of twenties rippling
in a soft, green fan ~ *plllrrr.*
It bulges, making him twice the man.
For seven days, he's a Puerto Rican Santa ~
medicina para Alma, a Key Food bag stuffed
with Oscar Mayer turkey meat, Wonder bread, munchies,
a Game Boy for Rafi, high-top Reeboks for Solo . . .
Okay, maybe not Santa . . .
He squints at a sailboat under the bridge,
imagines old man Jesus with his seven loaves, arms
outstretched, as if he could feed them all.

RAFI

8:00 P.M. Angel grabs Rafi midrun in Freeze Tag,
under the silhouette of Howard Housing's projects
in ghost-dusk. *You take your pills? No.* Angel frowns. *Go get them.*
Rafi dashes up the concrete stairwell.

Some minutes later, he emerges: a kid,
untethered and free playing tag.
But Angel knows what lurks under car hulls,
Wolverine-clawed, waiting to snatch Rafi by his ankles
and drag him as prey into its lair. Angel stands guard,

hawk over nest, guarding his brother-prince.
After tag, he buys Rafi a ham sandwich and hot
chocolate at the bodega. And a sour apple Blow Pop for fifteen cents.
No, he thinks. *You can't take him yet. Not without a fight.*
I still need him, this side of the light.

PALOMA

Paloma's apartment is a way station of lost angels
tucked deep in Brownsville's Howard Housing's projects.
He slips in with dawn, ignores the little Jesuses
praying on sills, dead cousins stiff in army suits,
or pretty-in-pink tías framed on wooden walls.
Adobo steams the kitchen as Paloma stirs.
Paloma, his abuela, always readying
a hot plate for a hungry mouth, tucking her own griefs
into her netted bun. Angel shifts on the plastic-covered couch.
Stares out the barred window.
Plays Nintendo with Rafi till humid night falls. As he grabs his keys,
he asks Paloma with an outstretched hand, *Can you bless me?*
She kisses his forehead, gives him a *bendición, mijo,* instead of money.

NINTENDO

Rafi hunches forward,
murders buttons. His teeth bite

his lower lip, he snarls as he swings
Bowser 360 degrees into an abyss, green-
fire burning his glasses, he cheers, *Yes! I
beat him!*

Even the tv sings mechanical praise
and crowns him . . . *Before I go*

to the next level, he says, inhaling deep.
He cracks his boyknuckles and grins.
Hannah grins back, tousles his hair. *Good
luck, Rafi,* she says. *Yeah. I need it.* He smirks.

She winces. Outside, sunlight dies
slow while his wild sixteen-bit dream begins ~
she sits back to watch Rafi fight his dragon
with flicks of his small joystick.

PALOMA'S PRAYER

Blessed be my daughter, Alma de Jesus, mother of Angel,
Soledad, y Rafael . . . rest in peace, Scarface Willy,
once married to Angel's second cousin Jessie
who made the block's best pernil,

y por favor, disculpe a Tío Rafael,
un alcohólico y former Latin King released
from Rikers only two weeks before he gave el SIDA
to shy, long-haired Solibel,

who lives across the stairwell
from Angel's titi Bella;
bendito, they say she cries at night, well

after her three boys be sleeping,
God, watch over her please, as well
as Alma's baby, my last grandson, Rafi.

SECRET (HANNAH)

A pain so big I can barely understand it.
Talk with Angel? Yeah right.
But Rafi. Oh Rafi.
No turning back now. How? Once his fingers
locked round my neck & I galloped
him down Crescent, his giggles bubbling like soda pop,
once he made me peanut-buttered toast,
called me BananaFanaMomanaHannah, that's it.
I'm locked in. Not pity anymore,
or tenderness, it's too close,

this pain breaks me like old wishes.
He's my brother now too. And he's got a secret
tucked in his redblood cells and it hurts
to look at a kid & think about Death . . .

◆

it hurts cuz his hair sticks up funny when he scratches it, cuz
he burps the McDonald's theme song, battles dragons, opens
bodega doors for you like a little prince . . . it's disgusting
to look at a kid & think about his expiration date. You want to vomit.
And you want him to never vomit,
wanna give him every Marvel comic, every Game Boy,
every small happiness, wanna break Joey's arm for sucker-punching him,
but you gotta let him fall & fight,

hurt & cry & you must honor his plight,
cuz he doesn't wanna be babied,
he wants to Live.
So, you let him run, wild,
but corner-eye-spy him, less than a block away,
play older sis for a day.

◆

Angel, his eyes
go soft when he looks at Rafi,
even tho he talks hard like an older brother should.
Nah, girl, we never talk about it — what is there to say?
My little brother got AIDS? No word could change a thing . . .
he was born with it, he'll die with it, only question, when . . .
only solution, make his days as fun & gentle as we can . . .
and Rafi's so cute, ma, when he skips between us,
he says, Banana Hannah, Angel — can you fly me?
Please? Fly me! So, we gotta grab his hands and swing him
like a crescent moon, his laughter pealing,
again, again! We gotta lift him for two blocks
till our arms get sore, even when he wants
more, more, more!
So we gotta try ~ we fly him
till he almost grows wings, nena. Ay.
That kid makes my heart sing.

Buggin'

Ooh! Youse is kissing! Rafi shrieks, when
Hannah & Angel flop in bed. He peers up close,
watching from inches away.
Are you guys gonna get married?
Yes, Angel says, *now go away.*
Rafi disappears, comes back hauling
a waist-high mirror — *Look at ya'll! Look!*
He scrunches his face and moans . . .
two peanut butter jelly *sammiches*
sit messy on the dresser. *Breakfast!* Rafi grins.
I made it myself. Hannah takes a bite and kisses him.
Thank you, baby, she says. *You're so sweet . . . Nah,*
I'm a bug . . . I'm buggin', he says,
strut ~ hopping into the kitchen.

MONSTER

El SIDA. Angel calls it *the monster* under his breath.
At night, it spiders windows with a hammer.
Snatches Tío Demas, two cousins, his mother
from bed. Sucks air out their mouths, blows death

in ~ a grotesque kiss. Thins cheeks to rice paper.
A white moss crystallizes lips. Sores sprout: blossoms.
Wrist-veins, green stems.
Worst, it leaves a mother too thin to give one last blessing

to a devastated son.
Sometimes a man needs
to be held, no questions.

Hannah rubs his lower back in circles.
Her eyes soak in his slump.
I'll protect you, she wants to say, but can't.

RAFI'S VOICE

When I die I don't want to be buried
in dirt cuz I saw a kitten last week
dead behind the school fence —
and he had bugs and maggots all crawling

out of his ear into his eye —
white, tiny, eating him from the inside.
When I die, Paloma, put me in a box
and burn me in a fire like I seen on Channel 13 —

then take all my smoke and dirt,
all the small handfuls of me,
and climb the Empire State, Paloma —
climb it and throw me in the wind

so I can fly like those pigeons
who black the sky with their wings

ALMA'S VOICE

She's a keeper, I told Angelito, cuz the way
She play with Rafi, my littlest angel,
the way she laughs with him all day & doesn't tire
of his constant bothering and games.

She ain't a wild chile like me —
that's plain to see. He needs a good girl
in this too-tough world. One who will
treat him like gold. And I see —

the little things they do to please
each other — the sweets, the door openings,
the kisses and back rubs and holding hands —

it's cute. Even innocent looking to me. I like it.
He needs more sugar in his life. I pray one day,
they make a baby & he makes her his wifey.

S.O.S.

When does their boat tip over?
What swells cause them to lurch,
turn sick inside, deep in da thick of it?
Perhaps when she saw Angel's eyes roll back

in his head the first time, as he dozed off
in front of her ~ slow motion, sweet,
heartbreaking. His dad was a junkie,
strung out on that sleepy killa

and he left Angel's mom. Sometimes at night,
Angel would take flight, while she was aroused, alive,
awake, with makeup perfect, baby ~ hair gelled,
present & ready for Love ~ he left her bereft, ignored, unwrapped,

dozing in hard drugs, caught in a generational despair
& an addict's affair far deeper than she could bear.
What kind of papi can he be, when half the time, he's a zombie?
So quickly it erodes, her sandcastle fairy ~ tale fantasy.

SICK

They don't hear rivers running through walls anymore.
Stiff legs with curled toes, three

stick bodies rubbing for fire, for heat.
The landlord's ignored all seven complaints she

hurled into his blinking machine. Rafi
sleeps between them like a squirrel nestled in

                            an oak's hollow heart. Lately he coughs,
                sneezes up green phlegm. His pale skin greens; he's small

              and dying. Hannah and Angel feel a thin-edged pain
                      slice through them like razor cuts.

                  Crying, Hannah carries him piggyback again
                    to Wyckoff's emergency room. Rafi breathes

                        through a tube. Angel seethes.
                      Visiting hours over, but he refuses to leave.

TOOTHACHE

This time, it's for Angel. She holds his limp hand and cradles him
in the sick-lit, moaning room. *It's aiight,* she soothes,
thumbing pages over his head. *Romeo, that spoiled prince —*

he had it easy, she fumes.
He had the luxury of attending masquerades, engaging in sword play —
he never had to beg to fix a swollen tooth

at Wyckoff's emergency room because he
had no Medicaid. She lays Angel's throbbing cheek on her shoulder.

Blue plastic seats
steal any ideas of comfort. *All he had to worry about — the plain miseries*

of love, she thinks. She stashes her schoolbook.
Tousles Angel's hair, watches *Days of Our Lives* on a hanging tv.

SOLEDAD

Hannah's in the bathroom, fixing her curls for the movies
when the cordless phone rings. Soledad whispers,
You there? Hannah sits at the tub's edge. *Wassup?*
He came over to chill, listen to the radio, then . . .

he shoved my face in the pillow, boots still
on, and took me from behind, the way
I never did it. She sobs. *Bastard. Baby Daddy.*
He said, it's mine. It's mine. Hannah grips the chill

sink ledge to keep from trembling. *Ay, Soli,*
she says. *Soli Soli Soli.*

No one should ever do that to you, baby. He had no right . . .
So I'm back on the shit. Soli cuts her off. *I had to hit the pipe.*

Silence. *He's coming — I'm out.* Click.
Hannah's world shrinks: a knot of black, tangled hair down the sink.

GIRLS' NIGHT

They lounge around a plastic kitchen table, legs splayed
in humid heat — Hannah, Bella, Rosie, Soledad, Antoinette.
After twelve Coronas with limes stuffed down sweaty necks, the girls let
loose: about Louie shoving the barrel of a silver .380

down Rosie's throat, all fucked up on a cocktail of coke & weed,
how Loco bolted Suhayla into her bedroom, barring her
from Bushwick Night School. Hannah remembers
when she first met Loco, how he bragged about isotopes, his GED.

Bella confesses Duke once dragged her by her braids down Jefferson Street,
Soli, of getting her head pinned to concrete with Craze's new Nike sneaker.

Hannah winces. Visions of butterflies pinned to flatboard, feebly
pulsing rubbed-off wings. Suddenly, she feels vulnerable, weaker,

an orange rind split with a sharp nail.
Outside Bella's propped-open window, a bottle shatters into hail.

MILAGROS

Of all Angel's titas she meets, Hannah is most
spellbound by Milagros ~ Jessie's mom ~
a tough downtown lawyer by day, da bomb
bella boricua by night ~ with fly hot~pink boas

and thick black liner, who comes around once
in a blue, with her stunning morena girlfriend Destiny ~
they dance in Village balls & discos & live so wonderfully
free ~ it seems ~ free from boys who jail & hurt & insult with blunt

words & fists ~ they spread glitter & joy & tears & magic
when they come around, bring Barbie dolls for kids
& six-packs of Coronas to loosen up their stressed~out parents ~
they don't stick around for any drama, honey, just long enough to Bless ~

to make Hannah dream another kind of life ~
filled with more freedom, laughter, more fierce joy & happiness.

Turn your eyes from me,
they overwhelm me.

~ SONG OF SONGS

III.

Otoño
Fall

And fleckéd darkness like a drunkard reels
down Hart Street, while a long-fingered Winter steals
Alma's last silvery gasp — so Angel's left a motherless child with no path —

And you, dear Reader, in your loving home,
have you ever felt so deer-wounded or alone?
Like a stone leaping into the sea . . .
He's locked in, but he wants to break free!

For a spell, she grew a little angel in her womb,
but Gotham wasn't ready for a gift so sweet
& they didn't have money to make ends meet.
So hopeless, she gives up her & Angel's baby
& prays for her God to forgive her daily.

She finds out he cheated; she's left disenchanted,
so he tattoos her name on his arm, not to be lonely, or stranded
but branded for eternity — his lover's own cherished thing . . .
they cling to each other, fear what nights may bring . . .

GLOW (HANNAH)

My whole body's tingling down to my
fingers. Something in my tummy warm &
lovely as a foal, a light I can barely
contain . . . I feel . . . rapturous?
Water breaking through a vase. Chaos ~ a dancing star in me!

My belly, housing hot energy
sparked by sunsets, sad eyes, kisses . . . a living
thing made by Love. How miraculous? I veer
away from cars, smog, stop in to a fancy-lit
café on Tenth Street, craving

fresh lemon slices.
I wanna guard myself from city ~ evils — my body is wiser than me.
Young lioness, ready to rip apart
any beast. Is this what it feels like? Aigu, uma, is this how you glowed?

Was this private motherlove enough? This quiet-body bliss?
Tell me. What should I do? I bite my lip, soak blood in my napkin.

JOB HUNT

Forty-second Street. Home of the hand-pocket-hustle,
always a help-wanted sign strung on a smudged glass window.

Angel enters the low-roofed BBQ joint, Hannah in
tow behind, into a cigar-stained musk. Lamps frayed

with red tassels. He asks for an application; fills
it out at the bar table. A blank

look on his face. He fills in spaces slow as dust; she flanks
his side, hisses correct spellings. One waitress trips. She
spills her mug of dark ale watching them cheat,

fidget, stall. His right hand stutters d's into b's.
Hannah hisses, *Stupid.*

In ten minutes, Angel rips up his splotched paper. Exits.
She trails behind, wordless. They hail a taxi.

Inside, she sobs, loud. He cries, soundless.

HUNGER

he's so hungry he can't even think
a bag of chips for breakfast and only if he's lucky
angie will fix him
a plate of leftover pernil but it's chips

pizza most days plus a few sniffs
of that good old yeyo tired n broke
wired n broke drinking coke
sniffin coke he's sick of it ready to quit but shit

one day a week is not enough cuz
by monday he's down to quarter waters

from jaquelina's so angel dreams
of barbecued baby back ribs ordered at charlies
or a rough slab of twelve-oz steak
tender not tough

UMA (HANNAH)

I'm curled in bed, clutching a pillow,
stomach rippling. Nothing in the fridge
'cept peanut butter & beer. All of a sudden,
hunger collapses me.
Wanna week at home, uma's galbi chim,
seven plates of banchan, spinach, meluchi,
kimchee, kochujang, cucumbers, salmon head,
talking to her barefoot in the kitchen
while the fan chops smoke into ribbons,
or after, when I'm full, oily, bloated,
when I nest my palms over my gut & lull.
Rest like a hammock swing
under fading light before apa
comes home wheezing curses,
before afternoon sours like old kimchee.
Oh uma, I miss you uma-ing me.

BENI

Hannah yells at Angel
in front of Sady's brownstone
steps. They're shaded by maples,
but her voice carries. Beni
walks towards them, she clams up.
Ice flows in her veins.
Yo, what's the problem? he drawls.
I hear your mouth two blocks
away, up Harman.
It's him, she spits,
hands attacking air,
but Beni warns, *Chill, chill.*
Angel's a man, not a kid,
ma. Watch how you talk to him.

APA

Watch how you talk to him ~
Beni's words ring in her
hours later like a morning alarm ~
didn't she hiss the same thing
once to her father? *Watch
how you talk to my uma,* each word
a dagger . . . she brushes her teeth, enveloped
in quiet. Angel sidesteps as she enters the bedroom,
filling it with her buzz.
After all those years,
she thinks,

I'm becoming Him.
She sits alone, half-in-shadow,
half-in-stark-light.

COCAINE

He's on it bad again.
It darkens the petals

under his eyes. All luminous metals
mined from his skin.

He fails her ET test —

fingertip to fingertip,
she can tell when he's high
cuz his blood throbs into hers
like trainwreck — one hot, wired mess.

Motherfucker! she spits.
What the fuck. She hurls a shot glass
across the linoleum. It splinters into bits.

At night, she sleeps with her back
to his bottle-hard

dick. Both of them
ground to shards.

She hears stories. Sometimes, her sweet Angel
is not an angel, when his boys circle up
to share tales of bravado, of wilding out
on the trains ~ she stays on the fringes

of conversation, hears scraps of details
that make her arm hairs rise — *He's a fighter,*
Googie says. *When I got jumped by those*
Nietas, only Angel came to my side —

It was eight to two, but he rammed that sucka
with a screwdriver in his side, knocked
another one's front tooth out — ooh,
flaco's no joke, they laugh. She cringes

to hear such brutality, she doesn't like
what it takes to survive in the streets,
Why? Why do you do that shit? she asks.
I do what I gotta do to survive, he says simply.

GODLESS

Because of one mistake —

no food for breakfast, the girl forgot to say —
she must stay awake while they

suck, scrape the baby.

Small walnut. Hardens, turns
her back on the world. Nurses

her hole. Black canyon. No one tell her
shit. Don't speak. Leave. Over-

head lights green, pallid.

Emptied of godlight. Girl blight.
Nothing divine. But one nurse sops
sweat from her forehead, stands by
the iron bed.

Grips tight her hand.

◆

Outside, they shake signs at her —
half-formed fetuses, spilt. Curdled.
An urge to murder them.

Bash feathered hair on concrete. Tell
them what she knows —

No one wins, ever.
The sky gray, indifferent.
Taxicabs roam;

stray mongrels.
She hails one down,

climbs into its rancid mouth.
Rolls down window.

Watches buildings blur.
Nothing moves inside her.

◆

God, I wanted to live so
hard. To feel my body race.
Bleed. Fly. Instead, I kill the
best things inside me. Why,
God? And what curse awaits
when I'm twenty-five, thirty? What

scarred, dry belly . . . my
future, a curled leaf . . .
I'm scared. Nowhere to turn
but inside. Smaller. Smaller.
Trying not to burn anyone else
with my dumb, hot touch.
God, why won't Angel turn
gold? Why ash?

Nas

Nobody knows we exist,
she whispers in the dark.
Your kind, my kind. They think you live to
steal cars, I live to sell beer & cigarettes.

Hannah feels liquid,
as if she might evaporate if she doesn't cling
to Angel's luminous ribs.
So? Who cares? he says,

stroking her messy hair.
I care. I care.
She pouts. He sighs & sings a Nas lyric —
like a blue smoke ~ ring, it halos the air.

Whose world is this? The world is yours . . .
He turns to sleep. She eyes the darkness.

Paradise (Angel)

It's no use.
Never good enough.
Never smart enough.
No matter what I do.

She'll never keep a baby of mine —
all my boys — Sitta, Googie,
Craze, Flex, Beni, alla
them got sons — only me left behind.

With this college girl and her mouth —
blah blah blah.
And her hard, little fists —

she knows I won't smack her, so I bounce —
out to Paradise, on Wilson & Starr, where
Joey waits with a wet kiss

◆

We split a gram,
take two long hits
till stars inside the room get
dizzy and spin

My heart's punched out. It beats
triple-time, a black punching bag
knocked into a blur. I
drink six Coronas as she

licks my neck.
My dick is stiff as
a soldier; it tents
my Guess jeans. But my lips,

my hands, my soul — all the rest
of me is soft. Dead. Limp.

No one told me — even tho'
all these bitches probably knew —
I had a feeling ~ the way
she was watching us, laughing a
little too loud as I sat on Angel's
lap in Maria's kitchen,
I pinched him hard on his thigh,
he pinched me back — some
private fight about nothing — but
she caught it. Her eyes on our thighs.
Later, outside, I shoved him
against a brick wall, piss-drunk, and lied —
I know, I know what happened —
he stayed shut, but it spilled

out his guilty-as-fuck eyes.
Admit it! Admit it, you
liar — I punched him
once, twice, a hundred times
on his chest, my fists numb,
then dropped to the curb
& held my chest so it wouldn't
break, rocking, rocking,
til I was sure I was still
in one piece. That night, street-glass
glittered extra hard. I was

A dead star. Alone in the universe.
Went back to Maria's,
called up the window —
guess who? this puta waves from the sill,
grinning! Espera, she says, runs down
the staircase. I corner her,
grill — Qué pasó, Joey?
Qué pasó con Angel? Díme. She plays dumb.
Angel, mumbling, ella sabe, ella sabe.
I stood so close I could smell her stank breath,
could smash her sweet face with my fist,
but I wanted to give her
one chance to be decent,
gimme an answer — instead,
she stutters, no sé, no sé,
then runs upstairs. I give chase,
she hides behind Maria,

lacing her Reeboks, all of a sudden
this bitch gets brave, talking bout
voy a matarte, China —
I said, vamos, let's do this —
and only his tías keep us
apart, splitting the door frame
with their arms, saying

nah, nah, it's late, nena ~
kids are sleeping ~ and this

worthless cabrón is standing
there, dumb-mute,
unable
to do shit about
this mess he started.

GIRLFIGHT, POSTFIGHT

Hannah twists her hair into a tight, low bun.
Flicks off her hoops. No earlobes ripped in two.
Joey stubs out her Newport against the brick
wall, crippling it in a hiss of spark and ash.

Angel's cousins tighten round the girls like a
noose. Bella offers Hannah Vaseline and sneakers.

She refuses: what will scar will scar.
Duke coaxes, *You better than her. Don't*
stoop. You got a house, you got a car.
Hannah spits — *Duke, fuck a house. Fuck a*
car. Last night, she stole my Heart.

Bella blinks, Angel stares.

The girls strut. Circle. Claws out. Sharp-
beaked, they clash — a whir of red, furious wings.

◆

After the fight, Hannah rubs raw aloe
on the lightning welt down her cheek.

A smudged mirror reflects a plain, scarred
face. Like a cratered moon. Outside,

Angie and Joey gossip, two shrill canaries.

Angel's tía yells *cállate!* over her telenovela's muted
violins. Hannah rides the ridge of her scar with her finger.
These are not my people, she thinks. How his tía watched
her fight like a gamecock, bet fives, took sides.
As if she were Angel's . . . thing,

a ten-karat ring slung on his neck.
Not a soul: tired, small, gleaming.

A scratched record skips in her head — *these are
not . . . these are not . . . my people.*

ENOUGH (POST GIRLS' NIGHT)

While other girls slump on couches,
hair slipping across cheeks, Bella & Hannah clink
Coronas into the sink. La Bella, Tía Bella, she winks
one Cleopatra eye at Hannah, then slouches
in the kitchen chair, tipping ash. Even with her stomach pouch
and thick arms, when she blinks slow,
she's glamorous as Vanessa del Rio. Hannah's face is pink,
flushed as blood in water. She kneads her creased brow.
It hurts. Bella leans over to stroke her hair
like a Persian cat. *You,* she croaks,
you got it good, girl. Angel, he don't stare
at other bitches all day, fuck around, or beat you. So
stick with him, mami. My nephew, she purrs. *He's a good kid.*
True. Hannah sighs. *But is he enough? For me?* she wonders, privately.
She drops her head. Rubs her eyelids.

DAWN

The next morning, a garbage truck beeps her awake.
Bushwick: a city of hangovers, sirens,
the diesel hum of too-early eighteen-wheelers. Hannah
watches a plane buzz by the window. It takes
eight seconds to disappear behind a brownstone. She shakes
her mussed head. Sunlight warms her hair, lends
her a red-brown halo. A brown wren
flits on the sill. She leans over Angel in sleep,
his body a thin rake, mouth slightly agape, open like an innocent.

It's this time. Before words. When the city is a blank sheet
waiting to be penciled in, when anything seems possible.
She grazes Angel's curly fro with her hand.
Sleeping, he throws his arm around her waist and sighs.

MIRROR

Hannah stares in the mirror, naked.
What is it that *She* has . . . what is it?
She touches a strand of hair. Too limp.
Oily. Her skin doesn't sheen —
it's a bruised peach under this light.
Her empty womb throbs.
Slumped shoulders. Sad breasts
pointed away like two dove's
wings, her hull-shaped
tummy . . . maybe
Her hair curls and gleams like polished scrolls of wood.
Maybe her nut-skin glows. A tight knot in her throat.
Nothing. Nothing about her shines
except her eyes. She swallows hard.
Blinks up at the ceiling to keep
her liquid light inside.

ONE

At Lucky's Tattoo Parlor, Hannah sketches the
blades of her name on tracing paper. 하나.

One. Meaning One Life. One Love. One Girl. One.
Scribe presses wax against Angel's jugular.

As he readies needle & snaps on gloves,
Angel finds Hannah's hand. Squeezes.

He's a scared boy at the dentist,
she thinks, a wince of pity as Angel's sculpted jaw clenches.

He stretches the long apology of his neck.
Black drops, red blood. Black, then blood. Blackblood.

Scribe carves slow, steadyhanded, thick,
to Red Hot Chili Peppers' Under the Bridge.

Pen grinds. Scribe hums. Hannah sings.
Angel closes his eyes till parlor lights go dim.

DA BRONX

Hannah's face glows with a strange, eerie light
above the Xerox — thirty copies of a 250-page
deposition. She'll be here all night. She sighs. Working in midtown,
living in Bushwick, a crazy double life

she shares with janitors, secretaries, doormen.
In Brooklyn, blackbrownred boys
roam streets like wild game, every day is high
season for cops, every two blocks a hunt, a catch, a kill ~

or a cage ~ lock 'em up, throw 'em away . . .
Yesterday, Gina, an Italian paralegal who chain-
smokes by the fire escape, said there's an opening in her building.

Good people, she puffs. *Nunna that crazy shit.*
Up in da Bronx, way up, on the #6, one bedroom.
Hannah dreams about it on her ride downtown.

APT.

Got it with her good credit!
One bedroom. Carpets, not wood.
Oh well, can't have everything.
Right off the #6.
Up, past the hundreds.
An hour from the city.
Forty minutes on the express,
Gina offers. A lifetime
from Bushwick.
Hallelujah! Yeah, there's drugs
& madness up there too — Hunts Point,
etc., but Angel don't know those cats.
He only hangs with his crew.
October first move-in date. She can't wait.

ROLLERBLADES

A week before they move to the Bronx,
Hannah plans a picnic at Central Park.
If it's not too cold, they'll spread a blanket
on the Great Lawn,
eat turkey & cheese sandwiches
with Italian bread, then rollerblade
at Seventy-second Street, where people
bop & swing in jazzy circles
to big headphones. 3:00 P.M. A date.
She waits with her food-heavy JanSport
as skaters whirl & turn
in spandex blurs.
Dizzy. She smiles,
bright neon buzzing past her.

BULLET

For eight hundred dollars, Leo kills his brother-in-law
on a Sunday. Sun a switchblade
paring people to paper-thin slivers; they
squint, flash in the harsh light. Blaze, tall,

green-eyed, serenades Jessie on her stoop,
all *pero mami, escúchame,* while Leo plays cool diagonal
across Jefferson Street until he raises his heat.
His flint-hard face won't flinch as all

four shots—brrah-brrah-bbrah-brrah — instar
Blaze's bicep. Neck. Shoulder. Chest. Blaze's jaws open;
say nothing. Jessie covers her hair, screaming,
crawls behind the hydrant. Four slugs roll under Googie's car,

dead copper bees. Angel's fist eats
them like a Venus flytrap. He shoots like a bullet from the scene.

ARREST

Her stomach sinks. Beni says,
He'll be at Central
Booking, ma, or at the Seventy-fifth Precinct.
Catch him before they ship him to the Island.
Once again the ground
swells under her feet,
threatens to capsize her. She's
broke. Gives blood
to get cash, calls Soli a week later,
goes on an all-night mission
to find him. What kind of God won't
give us a minute's break before
letting waves crash down again?
Hannah talks
loud & fake with Soli,
but inside, her heart dull-aches.

BAIL (ANGEL)

It's 5:28 A.M.
They give me back my shirt, my
jeans, my Guess watch, and
Hannah
bails me out. She's taking me
home. Never knew I missed
the smell of her neck until
she hugged me.
Didn't know
I missed
so much.
Didn't know I loved the peach parts
of sky, like soft sighs in the
morning air.
Or the smell of roasted peanuts,
how it gets caught in the back of
my throat.
Didn't know I loved
windows giving back a
mirror when lit

with more sky, more sky
in every eye. I didn't know
I loved trees, all five of them
on this block, waving
leaves

like greenfingers.
I remember hiding
under one's shade while
papi stuffed a brown
bundle down my jeans &
kissed me on the forehead before
I ran to make his deliveries.
I didn't know I loved the
wind, how cool it feels against
my skin, pushing me when I run,

always running. I
didn't know I loved taxis.
God bless this girl, her easy
twenties. I didn't know I loved
my own room,
Mickey Mouse frames,
Puerto Rico flag, my
shirts, towels, torn, but mine.
Didn't know I loved her
feet, toes curling climbing me as
if I were a tree. Didn't know I loved
her hands, so small, we touch
to make a prayer.
My palms swallow hers,
tiny, beautiful hands

how soft, they touch
the sides of my face,
my temples, my twin peaks, my eyelids,
as if my face is a
loved thing. I close
my eyes so she
won't see ~
she kisses
my eyelids, undoes
each shirt button like a wish
and I let go, let her
keep opening,
undressing,
undoing

me

Until the day breaks
and the shadows flee,
turn, my beloved,
and be like a gazelle
or like a young stag
on the rugged hills.

~ SONG OF SONGS

IV.

INVIERNO
WINTER

"Turn your eyes from me, they overwhelm me," lover,
you, who once drank from my heart's cup of water,

we're both parched now. Sere & spent.
Tired trees bent, God, how fast the years went

like a sad movie you rewind again &
again to make sense of the chaos & the tragic end . . .

But unlike the trusty Romeo & Juliet,
our heroes don't commit suicide or surrender just yet

(though Hannah cries over her barren
insides and her fallen Angel, she still tries

to remember the words of Nina Simone's
man-cry — "I gotta lotta livin' to do before I die —

but you just do what you gotta do, my wild sweet
love . . ." for Self, for Life, for Ancestors above —)

Dear Audience, the sad truth is: Time passes
too fast but You, yes, You — Live and Love to the last.

WARM

Late November, they wait for the J train
on the swaying platform. Iron
poles shiver and stars glint like mica.
Angel's boot cracks a vein into a sheet of iced rain.

He shoulders a sharp-toothed wind
while coats shuffle into Al's Liquor
Shop, a stray pit barks, and his mother
lies limp in a sickbed in Bushwick.

I'm cold, Hannah says. Angel bends down,
blows breath into her palms. He kneads her fingers
and warms them in his cave-mouth.

God, so gentle, she thinks,
how dark, how deep his eyes.
Snow falls like white stars into his curls.

CROOKED

After she bails Angel out, Hannah finds out he's not home free.
Cops, they try to get him to give up the killer's name,
but he's no snitch. *So they planted two bags of coke on me, ma*
he says — *and they're threatening to put me away,*

to lock me up in rehab, for not giving up my tío's name.
He had scooped up the bullets to get rid of evidence
and got stuck with a wack deal — snitch on familia
and risk a bullet from Blaze in revenge, or cop a plea

& plead guilty to some shit he didn't do.
Really, how can a street kid prove
NYPD cop corruption? Hannah fumes.

She drops thousands of dollars, every penny made
from her new paralegal job, on his criminal case,
hires a balding lawyer who slides his hand

down her thigh after one lunch meeting & says,
Why are you blowing all your money on this thug anyway?
Come, have dinner on me. My wife is so fat. I'm lonely.

Disgusted, she leaves & sobs quietly on the 7 train
home, feeling far from grown & completely alone.

HEAT

Tonight, with Bella's busted tv spewing sick light
over her bed full of kids,
Hannah wants to rip open any face, spill
outside, tear the iron gate off, take flight —

take the kids and run. Or just run.
To Aibonito. Jejudo. Hell. Heaven.
Sitting there, watching sweet Maria dart, cackle, sniff
white lines above the toilet, she knows. She's not Soldier enough,

not Nun enough, not Flint or Dove enough for a lifetime of
poverty. She knows her skin will fleck off like lead paint,
she'll burn, tender-fleshed, the young ones are like the unassuming

heater pole in the corner, all saint-
like, innocent, but inside, seething — deadly.
She shoves open the bathroom window, lets out steam.

LIONS

She's astounded that he can get coke planted on him,
be arrested and picked up while on his rollerblades
on his way to Central Park ~ how cops can be
so racist & corrupt, but it's no surprise to him.

He sighs. She pounds her fists on pillows as she practices tae kwon do.
That night, Hannah dreams that Angel is a golden~maned lion,
in a sparse valley with sunglassed hunters in squad cars. The valley
is full of starving, lithe, regal lions the color of midnight, ocean, fire, gold.

And the hunters are armed with rifles,
and packs of white baggies that they plant on the hunted lions' pelts,
saying, *This one was wild, Sarge, on drugs. Run,* she tells him, *run!*

She's a voice in da wind. Through a haze,
she sees zoos ~ filled with lions, who turn into snarling inmates.

She sees how captivity makes
regal souls calm, trapped souls crazed.
Run, she says, *run, young lions!,* as she stirs & wakes.

MOONLIGHT

Even with thick-soled Timbs, Angel treads slow over Jerome's
black ice, careful not to twist his ankle on his way home to Alma,
plate of arroz con pollo balanced on his palm. But three hooded men bump him
in their hustle to Highland Park. Chicken meat slips off bone;

rice & beans scatter like orange vomit into snow.
Angel's alone, fuming. He rubs open the box cutter in his pocket,
thin breaths coming hard, fast. They eye him;
loom like one huge shadow on concrete.

A three-headed demon. *What? You got beef?*
The fat one sneers —
moonlight fills the gash in his
boar-neck. Shorty grips the muzzle of a handgun.
Angel backs off, stunned.
Is it moonlight in his eyes, or tears?

SHINE (ANGEL)

she's my shine . . .
in my dreams she's always walking away, into the arms
of somebody richer, whiter, smarter, better.
but I can't let her —
she's mine.

with her, I can let go of all this
shit — uncurl my hand from a fist
to a hand that moves quiet as a whisper.
when I lie down with

her at night under
sheets, it's my safest place — I lay down all
guns — I swear
there's nowhere else I want to be.
just here.

streetlight blue on her black hair.
nothing like her, anywhere.

HART STREET

Angel loves this hushed pocket of night,
after his boys drift into sea,

after customers sniff and shuffle away
with a fistful of his two-bit white magic,
when window lights switch off one by one
like blown-out candles or stars,

when he's alone on the corner of Hart,
under Jaquelina's Christmas bulbs

half-golden in dusky hues,
air cool against his eyelids, he walks in half-
circles, does a two-step, sings dancehall reggae in
a high falsetto alone to his skinny self . . .

he lights a Newport, stares down the street —
it burns a blue line into infinity.

CHESA

Outside, a bloodorange moon
spills grief over Bushwick's battered brownstones.
Same moon Hannah's mother studies on her porch
before unscrewing jars, preparing meat, & rosewood plates for an early morning chesa ~

seaweed soup, pared apples, rice, incense for ancestors to inhale.
On this ripe harvest night, her father buttons up the Brooks Brothers suit
(he has no occasion to wear it except for funerals), to bow three times in the gray
dawn, circle smoke with a silver cup of water, inviting ancestors to drink.

She wonders now, staring at a cold, moonlit city, *Would they claim me as*
their own? Or am I completely alone? Where will I go when it's my time to go?
To a blue graceland in the sky? Will I fly home to my uma's land?

Will they greet me when I arrive?
She feels she could die or disappear, and no one
would notice, except the moon, a bloodshot yellow eye.

Cuban Link

When his mother dies, Angel clings to Hannah like seaweed,
even pulls her in the death-limo with his closest family.
He pawns his prized Cuban link necklace on Wanda's staircase
to lace Hannah's wrist with a ruby bracelet.

She takes off work for two weeks, sleeps
at his cousin Sady's. He collapses in Hannah's lap
in the back of the Q16 bus. One night in November,
letting guards down like cheap slips, she asks

him how many times he's cheated. They're sixteen.
His lips set in a grim line, he says,
Yo, don't ask that question.

She leaves. He chases her barefoot and shirtless
down Jamaica Avenue. She throws off his bracelet:
it stays lost in a gutter, a soft red glint.

(hold me, please)
We're down to the marrow.
I kneel in the narrow
tub in front of Angel;
he lays limp — a broken
toy soldier, thin arms
battered by hot,
slashing water, down his stomach
in rivulets. I don't know
how it feels to lose a mother,
anyone so close to kin.
All I know . . . is how to slow
this fall of water,
open my arms. Let him in.

FUNERAL HOME

Why Hannah loves Angel is never more clear:
Flaco, Alma's last husband,
who stole Angel's Pepe jeans & new Sony camera
last time he was home, who left opened beers

piss-rank in the sink, who left Angel's mother a baby with HIV,
now lurks outside of Saint Bartholomew's funeral home, lupine,
ghost-eyed under lamplight. A crowd of home-
boys and homegirls from Hart flock close to see

Angel lose it — fists, blood, a midnight brawl.
The air is knife-thick. She can hardly catch her breath.
Angel, stock-still, walks towards him slow.

Stops. His lips twist.
He lets loose a cry. Hugs Flaco tight.
They sob into each other's thick wool coats.

RAIN

He's standing in the rain, she's crying by her door.
Early December. Japanese maple leaves stain the
wet gravel red. A sharp pain
cleaves her rib cage like a switchblade. The cheap floor

of her apartment is soaked. God, no more
mornings listening to the express trains
hurtle by, watching amber light wane
in seawaves on his back. A cheap whore

in a Mets T-shirt, she imagines herself through
his eyes. But what does she know?
He's soaked to bone; his collarbones store

pools of rain. He tries to sear a true
memory of her into him — Indigo. Broken. Aglow.
He's standing in the rain. She's crying by her door.

ANGEL'S REHAB SUITCASE

Guess jeans,
two Polo sweaters,
Hannah's folded letter,
Bic shaving cream,

five pairs of white socks,
Fruit of the Loom long johns,
black velour tracksuit by Sean John,
beeswax for his new dreadlocks,

five plain white tees,
two do-rags, one Goofy tie,
E-Z rolling paper for trees,

four cotton boxers (one fly
silk pair), one necklace of cowrie
shells, one scrap of blue sky.

Rehab

A scrape of metal chair on tile.
Sign-in. The portly counselor,
Mr. Wilkins, who prods your old
lover to sit up straight for your visit while

scribbling notes on a pad —
he doesn't know anything. Anything.
When he leaves the drab office, Angel clasps your
fingers in his dry hands. You hate rehab.

Its cigarette death-air. His stubble. Torn T-shirt.
Hair thinning to peaks on his forehead.
His eyes, shadows of his young eyes.

How they search you, hurt.
You gaze up at his bare temples instead,
afraid to stare back with less. Or with a lie.

GUILT

Try as she might, she can't envision
a future with him beyond Bushwick —
tethered with children, yoked by familia,
she cannot wait the eternity of Angel's sentence

while she's still in the full bloom of womanhood.
Guilt chews her insides, but she can
no longer hide from herself the truth
of their unraveling, how her love for him has

become stained by all the grit & grime, dimmed
by their troubled, turbulent time together.
She stays awake, sleepless all night,
trying to decide her future ~

to let go ~ go for her own freedom,
or cling on to his sinking boat.

COUNTRYLESS

Ay, they were two children lost
under the merciless glare of city lights.
A Corean and Boricua, diaspora kids,
brave enough to ride
underground trains like metallic waves,
just to catch da electric surge of a hug
from a budding red ~ gold love . . .

Throbbing. Hot. Burning.
When she met him, she felt the loneliness
in him call out to the loneliness in her.
If her pain folded up

like a tight virgin rose, his pain
pulled her in like a gaping black hole.
Quiet, proud boy. His honey~brown eyes.

She sees them as two kids hand-holding over a glittering street,
lampposts arching overhead like acacia trees,

young ones in search of a thornless bed to sleep.

SEEDS

Towards the end, her wishes for Angel grow
small and hard as a handful of dry sunflower seeds:
she prays he'll get his GED . . .
his baby brother, Rafi, will grow
tall as a beanstalk . . . all
AZT cocktails sure as magic potions. She prays
he'll find a girl eager to read him medicine labels,
job applications, maybe even poems. He'll fall
in love with this stranger, she'll birth him a healthy son
for all the ones Hannah could not, would not, carry.
A girl who doesn't hiss, scream, throw things,
burn his self-esteem to ash. Someone
who coddles him, a good girl he could marry.
But she hopes she'll always be the Queens girl of his dreams.

You and I. We remember different stories.

The past is a burning book.

I'm unlearning the fairy tale — Angel — letter by letter by letter.

A shiny boy, cheap as a coin. If I rub the gleam off, are you copper or gold?

Does it matter, if I hold you in my heart-pocket

as a girl~child holds an amulet? What are we to each other?

Magic that conjures joy, halts the loneliness.

A lucky penny pulled shining from an ear.

And, wait, something heavier comes out. Night-grief.

Ancestral grief. Being called out our names, the spic-gook grief.

Being robbed of our sovereignty, colonized grief.

Oceans from our motherlands, diaspora grief.

Being two separate islands grief.

Still. We glow gold. Two flames. Bright and brief.

Until morning breaks our spell, Angel,

I dream of you holding me in this forgiving light.

GOLD HOOPS

One day she will be brave enough
to venture away from her huge gold hoops & bodysuits,
from parroting her mean friends' laughter, or sitting on the stoop
for hours, trying to look half-fly/half-tough,

sucking on a sour apple Blow Pop,
listening to the boom boxes spit out hip-hop.
One day she will
look at her rough, scarred face
without her MAC eyeliner and stop

hating those young, haunted eyes.
I hope a slant of gold light will hit her cheek
just right, and it may come as a surprise

to her how fine she really is. Fabulous. Sleek.
Soulful — full of her own juju and mystique . . .
a rose fury! Gold lightning when she hits the street.

GIRLFISH

She's gone. Like a woman entering a pool,

her body erased with each step.
What's left? A gold shimmer.

Now where will a lost boy fish for angels?
Not in stained-glass or god-songs.

Yes, he is alone in his city,
sidewalks parched as desert.

Oasis: glimmer of girls by Kim's Nails.
Mirage: every girl, an empty glass.

The closer he gets, the more thirsty.
His vision wavers. He scans the river-street,

searching for a girl in the shape of a salmon,
one who can break his

surface with a wild hallelujah of water.

Epic

(What if Angel was a true prince, not a mere
street king? And Hannah, a princess instead
of the daughter of poor Korean immigrants
who painted nails on Queens Blvd? Would we

altar their love higher, deem it Epic?
A new legend to toss skyward to salt our
constellations, not one to ball
into a fist or chuck in the dumpster. Spic

n' chink, one might call them, from afar . . .
but peer closer: a soul and a soul.
He folds over her like a rosebud in sleep.

She traces her finger over his sad map of scars.
If America let them, would they spin fast & gold
as a Celia Cruz classic, lilting songs into the sea?)

SKI

Lucy in the sky with diamonds, he thinks
a song his mother used to sing,
diamonds tossed in snow wink
at him like these coy, bright-eyed girls on Hunter Mountain's summit.

He inhales the iced air, frost-trees,
and when he glides down the mountain's soft shoulder, his
tracks, his spume like speedboat on lake~water —
he is black dolphin! Sea hawk! Any fierce, finned, winged thing, he shears

air with silver limbs like god-scissors,
wind singing a pegasus aria in his numb ears.
This fast, he could outrace death! Or fling

himself straight into its stark eyes. Unafraid, he floats in midnight sky above
whitecaps, slopes, gravity his only compass, he's flying past fear
to a different music now — holy holy dark angel taking wing!

JACKIE ROBINSON EXPRESSWAY

The highway is a silver ribbon threaded
through a lush hair of trees. She gets lost in its curves,
its shushing becomes her night music.
She's older now. She drives one-handed.
She knows these turns, seen them all before.
No longer a wet-lipped girl fidgeting
in livery cabs with Dominican drivers
who reek of Brut cologne and wink into the rearview.

She rides alone. Until sky breaks open. A greening
light. An empty highway she rides between dusk and
dawn, distance and time, watching the sun anoint
treetops, watching eyes of dull apartments catch aflame.
She drives, a silent witness with no name.

Every time, it's like being born again —

SOUL

I can't believe you wasted so much time, Wanda sighs,
and Hannah remembers now, Angel's eyelids trembling
like sails when she rocked above him, a maidenhead
tied to ship's helm, hit by sprays of salt water, foam, lightning.

How loving him made her learn the world —
a girl moving her fingers against the rough Braille
of welfare, food stamps, Rikers, probation. Dim, dim,
it brightens then — Bushwick, her harsh-lit

classroom rife with his tiger-scent.
How loving him, she moved
from girl to flesh to martyr to dagger
to stone to water to woman.

Yes. Woman.
And would she call those years a waste,
or a small taste of heaven in a man ~ made hell?
Aigu, Wanda. You will never know my soul.

DESIREE

Years later, Angel finally gets with Junie's lil' sister ~ Desiree,
who had an eye on him since lil' kid days.
With Desiree, Angel didn't have to be "better" ~
or hide his "dirty" habits ~

he could be free ~
like he was when they hugged & screamed
& played Cocolivio together back
in the summer of fourth grade ~

they always chose to hug each other, those two ~
got three babies now, lotsa big drama love scenes too,
like when Desiree made him tattoo a dragon

over Hannah's name
to start a new story . . .

While he sat under da hot pen (again),
he realized he was scripting his life
with another woman now ~

◆

Desiree was tough, into sexy goth, punk, metal, & black leather . . .
she wasn't a runner ~ she was a fighter.

She would stand by her man
and live on her block with her familia forever

and survive da rock, crack, and heroin games.
She became his new ma, and in divine time,
they lived out their own chaotic, epic Legend.

(But sometimes, when Angel was alone & high,

late at night, after three blunts, two Coronas, & in a nostalgic mood,
he wondered where she flew off to . . .

she was too soft for New York, he thought ~
more of a Cali girl vibe . . . she hated

da bars on the windows everywhere in Brooklyn ~

Ugh. Looks like cages, she said, more than once ~
I gotta get outta here ~ it's too cold, too crazy for me . . .

◆

We have choices!
We have a right to live happy!
And I'm gonna carpe diem, yo,
by any means necessary!

Hannah used to proclaim, loudly,
dreaming of Berkeley and beaches,
shouting things at him crazily
while he grins, things

she wishes she could yell
at her pressure ~ cooker parents.
He wonders
if she has babies now too, or if she

just lives free as the wind still,
untethered & lost

as a golden ribbon
unraveling from a bouquet of heavily thorned, stunning roses ~

◆

He secretly wonders: What became of the golden girl
who whispered songs & rhymes into his ears
and wanted to become air?

Who inhaled & kissed his warm temples
and grazed his long lashes with the grace of a gazelle?

A young girl who transformed into woman
at dusk with his touch, swaying over him like coconut fronds,
riding him like ocean waves till he filled her with stars?

He felt, at heart, she was far, far away . . .
After he tattooed a dragon over her name,
he brought honey & white daisies
for the Goddess of the Sea
who Jessie told him is Yemaya ~
when the familia went to Coney Island,
he took a moment to walk out to where shore meets sea alone,
and silently asked the sea ~ goddess to watch over & protect

Hannah's many journeys as white petals
floated over water, fragile & lovely ~
slowly carried out by the rippling waves.
Por amor, mi amor.)

Desiree comes up behind him,
locking her arms around
his lean, rippled waist.
He lets out a deep sigh,

kisses the mother of his three
angels on her forehead,
takes her hand, and walks
with her back to their children,

whose little hands are busy
making a round castle in the sand.

PRAYERS

From lifetimes away, from islands apart ~ she still

wonders about her Angel as she holds a handful
of tiny, intricate shells in her hand ~ remembering
their summer days at Coney Island Beach,

she wonders if he's caught
still living a stoned ~ dream ~ haze
or awakened to the beauty & possibility in being alive ~

she still prays for him and his family ~ his children ~ the future generations
to inherit his heated, hunted, dancing blood. Wishes
him well from afar. And Rafi ~

sweet Rafi. Last she heard, he lives ~
lives on ~ loves on ~ so beautifully
into his teens. New medicines work miracles

daily ~ days & years continue on ~
& Hannah ~ she flies alone to a distant island
to birth a new story. A new bloodline. A new legend.

Acknowledgments

Aloha. I would like to express my deep gratitude to my dear friend Bushra Rehman for teaching these poems in her writing workshops, and to Nicole Counts for being the most brilliant, insightful, and compassionate editor I could ever ask for.

Deep gratitude to Chris Jackson, Victory, and everyone at One World and Penguin Random House who found beauty and truth in this story, for helping me bring this love to a larger audience, and to my amazing agent, Clare Mao, for believing in me & supporting my journey as a writer.

Special thanks to the amazing Kamilah Forbes and the talented DJ Reborn for helping me to bring *Angel & Hannah* to life from page~to~stage at the New York Hip-Hop Theater Festival, for allowing these poems to dance & breathe, and for creating a loving soundtrack for my sonnets.

Gomapsimnidah to Sunyoung Lee and Juliana Koo of Kaya Press, publishers of my first book, *The Temperature of This Water*. Saranghe.

Sarang to Theresa Hak Kyung Cha (rest in peace) & her work *Dictee*, which moved me deeply as a Korean American woman, a line of which ("a stone leaping into the sea") is loosely referenced in this novel.

Abrazos y amor siempre to Little Nelson Abreu, Nicky Nieves, Irma and Gloria de Jesus (rest in peace), y familia. To Karin Castillo, Mabel Tso, Celinda Casanova, Bianca Gomez, Fay, Wendy Cartagena, Jessica Cruz, Norlene Cayetano, Laarni, Natasha Netto, Kuem-Hee Rhee, Sze Pui Cheng, Sarah Ra, Zola Zakiya, Sonya Payne, and Jeanne Choi ~ my sisters for life! <3 Thank you for growing with me, ladies ~ saranghe. My love always to the Asian American Writers' Workshop for raising me, and to all the amazing artists, musicians, singers, emcees, and poets through space and time who have inspired me and have influenced my poetry and the writing of this novel. My deepest thanks to You ~

Toni Morrison, Alice Walker, Sonia Sanchez, Joy Harjo, Ntozake Shange, Jessica Hagedorn, Arundhati Roy, Maya Angelou, Eric Gamalinda, Oliver de la Paz, Ai, Nas, Lauryn Hill, Oprah, Yasiin Bey, Black Star, Talib Kweli, Kuttin Kandi, Dave Chappelle, Chris Rock, Richard Pryor, Tiffany Haddish, Eddie Murphy, Charlie Murphy, Prince, Ali Wong, Bao Phi, Tina Chang, Jeff Chang, Ed Lin, Alexander Chee, Robert Sullivan, Nick Carbo, Patty Kim, David Mura, Li-Young Lee, Christy NaMee Eriksen, Cathy Park Hong, Emmanuel Ortiz, Momo Chang, Sheng Wang, Joan Osato, James Kass, Lee Herrick, Rain Noe, DJ Boo, Jasmine Choi, Giles Li, Malaya Arevalo, Sonam Wangmo, Hisae Kato, Felicia Hill, Peter Ong, Parag Khandar, Jen Alvarez, Sham-e-Ali Nayeem, Terry Park, Taiyo Na, Sarah Ha, Dennis Sangmin Kim, Danny Thien Le, Sandra Cisneros, Nick Carbó, Breyton Breytenbach, Eileen Tabios, Kristina Wong, Lois-Ann Yamanaka, Sade, Lee Tonouchi, Ed Bok Lee, Edward Garcia, Jeannie Wong, Darshan Mendoza, Jade Rajbir Kaur, Kumu Dane Silva, Kumu Ehulani Stephany, Otis

Redding, Aretha Franklin, Bill Withers, Sam Cooke, Bob Dylan, Bob Marley & family, Jerry Seinfeld, John Lennon, Sean Lennon, Yoko Ono, the Beatles, Digable Planets, Nice & Smooth, Shabba Ranks, Black Moon, Black Sheep, Biggie, Russell Simmons, Stan Lathan, Run-DMC, Mary J Blige, Tupac, Beyoncé, Solange, Alicia Keys, Jessica Care Moore, JLo, Janet Jackson, Faith, Shakira, Norah Jones, Carla Bruni, Ben Harper, Jack Johnson, Steven Tyler, Bret Michaels, Jon Bon Jovi, Sebastian Bach, Björk, Opensouls, Kyu, Jay-Z, Fat Freddy's Drop, Katchafire, Common Kings, Alex Marley, Joan Baez, Joni Mitchell, Adele, Moby, Beck, Jimi Hendrix, Led Zeppelin, B. B. King, Fania All Stars, La India, Jerry Rivera, Celia Cruz, Elton John, George Michael, Erasure, Sublime, Bill E-Fluid, Liam de Koster-Kjaer, Mike Hall, Whitney Houston, Nina Simone, Willow Smith, Jada Pinkett Smith, Andre Merritt, Chloe Flower, Madonna, Jane Kim, Beau Sia, Saul Williams, Paul Flores, Chinaka Hodge, Snoop Dogg, Marc Bamuthi Joseph, Pops Mohamed, Chiwoniso Maraire, Maisey Rika, Spike Lee, Issa Rae, Ana Duvernay, *Flight of the Conchords*, Suheir Hammad, Tamika Harper, Lemon Anderson, Leanna Zuniga, Amelia Perez, Amalia Leticia Ortiz, Mayda del Valle, Black Ice, Staceyann Chin, Flaco Navaja, Poetri, Shihan, Bassey Ikpi, Lynne Procope, Eric Thomas Guerreri, Steve Cannon, Willie Perdomo, Mervyn Taylor, Kamaui Braithwaite, Cheryl Boyce Taylor, Ta-Nehisi Coates, Shakespeare, Petrarch, Elizabeth Barrett Browning, Emily Dickinson, Walt Whitman, Regie Cabico, Fish Vargas, David Velez, Amy Tan, Maxine Hong Kingston, Lara Stapleton, Anne Carson, Paule Marshall, Eileen Myles, Susan Ito, Yuri Kochiyama, A Tribe Called Quest, Kimiko Hahn, D'Angelo, Raphael Saadiq, Landon McNamara, Hirie, Pharrell, the Last Poets, Cristin O'Keefe Aptowicz, Shappy, Bob Holman, Jason Mateo, Jason Bayani, Jocelyn De Leon, Ani DiFranco, Rich Ejire (DJ Flood), André 3000, Outkast,

Paula Fuga, John Cruz, Cree Summer, Cecilio & Kapono, the Beamers, Anuhea, the Lim family, Ammon Tainui Watene, George Kahumoku, Country Comfort, Israel Kamakawiwo'ole ~

You have influenced my style, sense of beauty, truth, & cadence. Your art has blessed my life. Mahalo nui loa.

To the loves who have blessed my days & nights ~ forever grateful for You sharing your Spirit with me. A part of You always lives in my heart ~ You are a special song in the soundtrack of my life ~ mahalo nui loa for sharing your aloha. Saranghe.

To Hawai'i — whose waters, wonders, songs, spirit, & aloha still humble & amaze me & give me new Life ~ Forever grateful. Mahalo ke Akua. Aloha ke Akua.

My ancestors. God. Jah. Allah. Buddha. Akua. Our Creator.

To the goddesses ~ Saraswati, Hi'iakaikapoliopele, Pelehonuamea, Kuan Yin, Atargatis, Isis, Ixchel, Yemayá ~ for your sacred magic & beauty.

To my Korean American and Asian American communities. For nurturing, supporting, & sustaining me.

To my parents for giving me Life. For raising me. Forgiving me. For loving me. To Kunemo. For Inspiring me. To my cousins. For the good company. To my grandparents. For watching over me, still and always.

To my brother, for surviving me, and for surviving with me. Saranghe. Gomahwuhyo.

To my daughters —
my life's sweetest blessings —
Sulei Bada Hiva Kai'a Xaxa
&
Senai'a Atarangi
~ Saranghe ~

To my first love
to all first loves
to all lovers
to all love
to love
love

∿

ISHLE YI PARK is the author of *The Temperature of This Water*, published by Kaya Press. Her first book is the winner of an Asian American Literary Award (Members' Choice) and the PEN Open Book Award. Her poems have appeared in publications such as *Ploughshares, Mānoa, Barrow Street,* and *Century of the Tiger: One Hundred Years of Korean Culture in America.* She is the first woman to become the poet laureate of Queens, New York. She lives in Hawai'i with her family.

ishleyipark.com

ABOUT THE TYPE

This book was set in Vendetta, a typeface designed by John Downer as an homage to the advertising signs painted on walls of old factories and warehouses of roadside America. Downer began his career as a journeyman sign painter, and Vendetta was inspired in part by the brushstrokes used in sign painting, which give this typeface its distinct angular character.